THE
WORST
THAT
COULD
HAPPEN

FUNGASM PRESS
an imprint of Eraserhead Press
PO Box 10065
Portland, OR 97296

www.fungasmpress.com
facebook/fungasmpress

ISBN: 978-1-62105-299-9
Copyright © 2019 by S.G. Murphy
Cover art copyright © 2019 Eraserhead Press
Edited by John Skipp

Printed in the USA.

THE WORST THAT COULD HAPPEN

S.G. MURPHY

For my brother, Jack.

CONTENTS

SHIT JOBS OF THE HORRIBLE FUTURE

A WILDLY ENTHUSIAST INTRODUCTION TO THE CYBERSPLAT SHENANIGANS OF S.G. MURPHY: DOOM-PEDDLER-AT-LARGE

BY
JOHN SKIPP

I've always been a fan of great science fiction horror, where the inevitable results of unbridled technological "advancement" bite us right in the shimmering tin-plated ass. There's a grim gallows-humor satisfaction in seeing smart, searing, immaculately-constructed dystopian scenarios unspool before our eyes, in an achingly unflinching and plausible manner.

The dream, of course, was that all this technology would actually make our lives better. And in many ways, of course, it has. Any caveman with a mouthful of magic mushroom heard the prognosticative psychedelic clarion call of a future far better than their primitive present, shuddering through their DNA. Where their sabertooth tiger steak didn't rot on the spot, but could be slapped in a fucking refrigerator. Where childbirth wasn't a death sentence for both mother and child. Where communication beyond grunts and large rocks slammed into their skulls resulted in the birth of intelligent thoughts worth communicating. All of that has been achieved, for large swaths of the human population.

But here we are, all the way into the 21st century. And for most people, the bulk of day-to-day life is still experienced as the shit end of the stick. We now work for the machines that were built to serve us. And the deeper we come to know ourselves, and the world/universe/multiverse we live in, the more painfully aware we are that the future ain't all it was cracked up to be.

So here's what I love about S.G. Murphy.

I met him as a student in my online LitReactor class, "The Choreography of Violence", where my job is to teach people how to write action scenes. This is a very specific set of skills, focused on precision, momentum, and emotional engagement. And you would be amazed by how many talented, accomplished writers *do not possess these skills*.

So in waltzes young S.G. Murphy, on his first assignment, with a story called "Tracking" (which appears herein). In it, this poor hapless joe is assigned to hunt down a woman on the run who is, shall we way, technologically enhanced. He and his buddy are well-armed themselves. But they have nooooo fucking idea what they're in for.

The story is, as you're about to see, spectacular. In a few short pages, he manages to a) build a ragged, wholly believable future, b) put us squarely in this weary working-class stiff's shoes, c) slyly bring us up to the moment of impact, and then d) unleash some of the most meticulously-detailed, insanely-escalating mayhem imaginable, every word a miniature wrecking ball pulverizing the one behind it in shattering chrome-and-redmeat sprays that dropped my jaw down to my toenails.

I think my highly-professional teacherly response was, "HOLY SHIT, DUDE! What ELSE have you got?"

The results are here for you to see.

When I throw out the playful term "cybersplat", I am of course referencing the cyberpunk and splatterpunk literary waves of the late 20th century. And yes, young master Murphy deploys both the scrappy subversive futurism of the former and the wily taboo-shattering transgression of the latter. In the process, he also doubles down on the pure punk attitude of youthful rebellion and prematurely world-weary, bird-flipping resistance to the crushing weight of the powers-that-be.

I'd also like to point out that – in keeping with Arthur C. Clark's maxim that "Any sufficiently-developed technology is indistinguishable from magick"—there is a whoooole lot of mystically mindbending madness radiating from the core of these stories. Did he just call those guys "angels"? Did that plant just grow a face and eat you? Religion is old-school, and its relics remain; but the spookily spiritual dimensions unleashed by said technologies might make us wish we'd never opened the goddam door.

The book you hold in your hands is deceptively slender. But please allow me to assure you that every single story here carries a novel's worth of payload, in terms of world-building brilliance, crispness of character, and dizzying plot development. These stories are densely deep, deep dives, compressed down to radioactive diamonds that mutate your brain as they explode on contact.

And through it all, you'll never be able to forget that in another century or so – if we still exist – we'll still be driving to work and cursing our jobs. Doesn't matter if you've got an android head. Doesn't even matter what planet you're on. You'll still be taking whatever the new drugs are, to cope with the new world's stresses. You'll still be wildly underpaid, as part of the 99%.

And you'll dream nostalgically of the good ol' days, where you could just read S.G. Murphy's THE WORST THAT COULD HAPPEN, instead of actually living it.

What's the worst that could happen? You're about to find out.

ENJOY!!!

Yer pal in the palpable present,
Skipp

THE MADNESS OF MORAY MOON

It always feels a bit like vertigo.

Gravity inverts and lands him on his feet, a metal platform smothered in cream-colored clouds and whipped bare of rubbish by the winds of gas giant Ordovan Prime, here in the Gevurah Dimension.

She'd sent him.

Wait, did she, or did he pick it up himself?

Goddammit, was this a point-and-click, or an *assigned contract*?

Door system always ruins his equilibrium.

Interdimensional hitman extraordinaire Dutch Schultz rubs his face with one scarred and calloused hand. Though the face isn't any more lined than that of a working man in his early thirties, he's starting to show his age to those close enough to know it. His neatly parted hair has turned completely jet black. At least sixty percent of his original body is gone, replaced with the mechanical and the techno-organic. He continues wearing thick framed glasses, though instead of fixing his sight they read him things like his pulse and his bank account, bounty lists and odds of survival.

It's a typical scene of the era—dingy neon lights on very few of the formerly-silver mine gantries, wind-fans long run to irregular loops, the prefab hovels and monitoring posts crumbling and rusting into lean corpses. Wide catwalks for aglaotinum trolleys with pedestrian lanes connect platforms and refineries, the hungry sky beneath every step at vigil for the unwary. Palace of the damned, an ashen monument to the once vibrant universe, now eerie silent save for the hedonistic cackles of reprobate nightgoers. An enormous moon casts its baleful glow from the east, taking up a large portion of the blue expanse, bright and beautiful and terrifying.

Nobody mines aglaotinum on Ordovan Prime these days, not for near a century now.

Despite the wind, he's not cold. Rourke-6 IBR subdermal combat skin, baby; temperature regulation at the flicker of a neuron. Schultz's black suit thus doesn't feature a coat, his vest buttoned over his tie, sleeves rolled up. Constellations of scars and tattoos, mystic ink and knots of tissue cover the slender muscles of his arms and torso.

A few pouches run across the front of his belt, itself attached to a leather shoulder holster situated comfortably under his left arm. This cradles his beloved Colt automatic, the massive murder engine sitting cozy where it was during his time in the Somme and again in Manchuria, his days in Cartagena and nights in Samarkand, dawns on Myrol IV and dusks on the paradimensional Nethercroth Express. He feeds this cannon custom forty-five caliber slugs cast from melted silver meteorite and the nails of three-century-old coffins—gotta be at least a century but anything over three is best. Baby girl slings said missiles down a barrel scored with righteous carving. A bolo knife with similar modifications sits strapped to his right thigh, a blessing from New Siquijor.

There is very little these can't kill.

There is very little *he* can't kill.

In short, he's a sight himself, a pale horror lean and sinewy loping across the mausoleum of Ordovan's former glory, bearing down on his prey.

What a contract it's looking to be.

A local syndicate known as the Borderline has contacted the Foreman. Whether it was a standard-entry contract or a fully fielded prayer, Dutch doesn't know, but he knows the request urgent enough to require his attention. A low-level lieutenant in the organization seems to have broken away with her hands on some interesting technology, carved out a nasty little bit of turf.

The description of the engines acquired gives Dutch a furious déjà vu—sounds like the woman is consorting with his oldest and most loathed foe, the Kindred of Tubal-Cain.

According to the skim, though Moray Moon herself began life as a relatively standard descendant Ordovan, her last known appearance was *very* posthumanoid, remote even to our favorite transhuman hitman—star-tan skin dense with wires, the bone structure humped and warped. Shark-toothed and black-eyed—a textbook Vampire. She wouldn't be more than a violent curiosity, an isolated planetary problem suitable for spring cleaning, if Moray hadn't begun using the old machines to "spread the word" beyond Ordovan.

Ashfield Colony was lost entirely, their frozen corpses formed into the Foreman's sigil in the cold tomb of their own pocket dimension. The Watchtower at Subeth managed to get out a single SOS before disappearing. Dutch can't recall if it was a prayer or an emergency alert. He only remembers the recorded aftermath—Subethi bones as candlesticks, alien names listed on the wall in their respective fluids.

Schultz lights a spliff and strides across a railed catwalk buckled with pressure.

At the disc ahead an internal elevator should take him to a tea parlor called Lost Time, where the few remaining members of Borderline wait to abet his contract. Towering stacks of commercial stalls linked by stairwells dominate a quantity of Ordovan's mining town, casting color into the night where operable. The internal elevator is a wire caged affair that looks like it might burst into pieces at a footstep but with a sputter it heaves him into the upper discs.

Lost Time has a stylized sea-foam sign flickering with blown fuses. Past the gambling tables and the tea booths he opens a black door that blends with the wall and enters as it clicks behind with a whisper.

A slender man a head shorter than Schultz in a greatcoat and fine navy suit, his eyes hidden by an enormous pair of blindered sunglasses, stands from the rounded table and presents a hand. Schultz takes it in his own enormous clammy claw and pumps the arm. "Mr. Shimamura, I presume."

"Mr. Schultz. There was no exaggeration on your guarantee of promptness. Very respectable to see these days."

Dutch nods with a mineral smirk. Shimamura gestures to the other two people seated at the table. "This woman here is my remaining capo, the elder gentleman my advisor Durand."

Schultz shakes hands with the woman—Yaneska—built like a brick shithouse, the old man Durand trembling with some sort of neurological disorder. Regardless of ties Dutch immediately can see how easy it would be to kill all three. A force of habit that's hard to break.

Durand's voice is a croak to match his look. "If you have any outstanding questions, you can field them before we begin. Mr. Shimamura and I discussed there were likely holes in our request."

"How are there living sapients on Ordovan?" Dutch's scratchy bass owns the room when he speaks as if linked to a subwoofer.

Durand gives a crinkly smile. "Think the answer's in the question. Moray may be using the remaining people here as cover, perhaps even shields. There's certainly no one left to oppose her in force. Borderline is down to us three."

"We may even be a launchpoint," offers Shimamura, lighting a cigarette. "A pantry. The Ordovans will help sustain her if forced to flee retribution."

"By sustain..."

"Yes."

Yaneska looks up from the table. "There's something else."

"There's a lot else," laughs Shimamura.

"He needs to know how she's doing what she's doing."

Shimamura's face tanks. "Yes, absolutely certain." He turns his chair directly to face Dutch and crosses his legs. "We felt you and your employer were the right contact based on our experience with her mutiny."

Durand is shaking his head. "Here it comes."

"She's long been dissatisfied with operations in our syndicate, long campaigned to take charge herself. She's now requisitioned a gunship of some sort, a heavily-armed orbit-breaking space-capable craft. I've never before seen anything like it and I don't know where she found it."

"Like something from a deep ocean. Sharp. Horrible-looking."

"These weapons, they're—"

"The condition of contemporary bodies—"

"Like they were flayed by a hot dull knife."

Dutch Schultz has been clenching one fist during this exchange, the knuckles white. He inhales deeply and flexes the fingers. "Let me guess. She seemed dazed, hazy constantly after some indeterminate time—"

Yaneska's eyes narrow.

"—and now she doesn't even look the same anymore, yeah? When was the last time Moray Moon was seen?"

"About a week ago."

"How'd she look? To you, I mean."

Durand spits on the floor. "Like something else was living behind her face."

Dutch nods. "Let's hear your briefing on the contract proper."

Moray reaches into her own throat and yanks out the mouthpiece of an old crank telephone.

"Engage."

In the dark of the ancient aglaotinum mines, ancient furnaces and boilers flare into activity, cycling the stink of rotting flesh through dead and dying rooms.

Eyes flicker open, gears begin to churn, and the black exhaust of tortured minds laughs itself into activation.

Durand sighs. "It's a much older part of the facility but we've determined some sort of reservoir down there is by far large enough to hold a skyworthy craft. Our attempts to clear the way when we had force of population were successful only to the point that it kept them from getting a foothold up here. We figured we did a lot of damage, but that's obviously not the case."

Schultz nods. "They resemble your former comrades, yes?"

"Uh, well, more like if someone flayed our former comrades and draped their empty skins over an ill-fitting metal frame, but yes, loosely. No pun intended."

Dutch grinds his teeth. *MotherFUCKING Necromatics.* "Would you like a memento?"

Shimamura blinks a few times.

Durand coughs into his fist. "Excuse me?"

"Some clients like a memento, for proof or personal keepsake, of their target. Ear, finger, weirder things have been asked."

The table is silent.

Yaneska finishes her tea and fixes Dutch with a steely glare.

"I want her head."

"Yaneska, Christ."

Schultz nods. "Consider it done. Condition is no guarantee."

She nods back.

Durand stands, brushes his coat off, excuses himself to the restroom. Shimamura coughs and places a cigarette case on the table. Next to it he drags up a footlocker. "I understand you and your employer take a rather unusual form of payment, Mr. Schultz."

"As was indicated."

Shimamura opens the cigarette case and unfolds a long thin slip of carboned receipts. "We've made it a point to obtain the items asked for. Asteroid minerals are, of course, difficult to come across without the mining expertise...hazards, you understand...we *were* able to acquire the full payment. However, I do think you may want to consider your clients' economic position in these cases."

"We do." Schultz glances over the receipts—scrap electronics, a psychoelectric turbine, ten thousand old credit dollars' worth in meteor silver. He checks the case and then both he and Shimamura sign the slip. He taps the footlocker. "I'll come back for this. I trust none of you are stupid enough to try and stiff us."

As they stand to leave Yaneska holds an arm out. "Listen."

No longer can they hear clattering saucers, exchanged money, hushed chatter. The tearoom is silent. Shimamura nods at Yaneska and opens his coat; Dutch draws the Colt and holds it against his cheek.

Yaneska opens the door, pulls Durand's body in with one arm, shuts it. The old man is already dead, blood leaking from the shirt as his skin slides off beneath her hands. Something slams against the door and Schultz, knocking a chair out of the way, puts a foot on it and fires the Colt through but once, a thunderburst in the black tea room followed by the *tink* of an empty casing. He opens the door and gives something a violent kick.

What patrons were unable to flee have been liquidated, their melted corpses left with ribs agash and faces screaming, draped dripping across the shattered china of their tea tables with limbs splayed. A Necromatic is on the ground, internal gears grinding to a tormented halt, the human skin draped over it leering with a hollow grin. Smoke bubbles from the chest furnace.

Dutch crouches down. "Think you got too close to the door."

He holsters his gun, about-facing to Shimamura, who stands

with lips pale and narrow. "Your old friend is fucking around with shit she doesn't understand."

"What is it?"

"Evil technology. Ancient."

"I'm not sure I understand."

"I'm not here to explain everything, but your Moray's a Vampire."

The last two members of Borderline stare vacantly.

"A living person willingly implanted with the demon machines of the Kindred of Tubal-Cain, instruments usually reserved for corrupted dead. The name makes sense since the converted feed on the blood and flesh of living beings. Usually sapients."

They continue to stare vacantly.

"I'm gonna walk down to that hangar and kill every single Necro -*fucking*-matic I can get my hands on. Then I'm going to carve your lieutenant's idiot head off."

Dutch spits on the dead machine on his way out the door.

Shimamura turns to Yaneska and offers her a cigarette. "I imagine depending on his speed, they may come for us soon. Certainly they will if he fails."

She takes a long drag and shrugs. "I'm not super invested anymore, boss, I really have to be honest."

"Neither am I."

If there was enough of Moray Moon left, it would be able to remember the start of this.

But what she's become can barely remember the month before contact.

The mounting self-centered frustration, the anger, a narcissistic fixation on running the show and the confusion at why she wasn't, she who was so much better than the others.

Traits that catch the Tubal-Cains' attention.

It started with dreams of her fellows falling apart, struggling to hold their limbs together, pleading with her to call for aid, to help them be better. Weeks waking in a cold sweat, clutching her temples, nervous capos checking the door with sideways eyes. When she gave in, crumbled and begged to know how she could find the help she needed, she saw every enforcer under her command genuflecting, her right hand raising his arms as if to offer her something.

"Skin us," he pleaded.

Everything got clearer after that. She fasted for three days and three nights and then, still soaked in her own urine, skin them she did—though they begged for her to stop, her knife was inexorable, for they'd most certainly demanded to be flayed, hadn't they? Just testing her devotion, perhaps, seeing if she were truly committed to helping her Kindred.

She had one final dream. A pale and emaciated thing, a corpse really with a rotten shroud of canvas draped over its warped head, the cloth humping and bunching in places alien to human physiology, a broken halo of jagged metal lurching drunkenly above. It twists and warps in the air before her, broken limbs too long, body decomposing and cancerous. In a voice as mechanically grating as it is crooningly alien it calls itself Brother Candriel.

Whose brother?

Yours, my dear, my darling. Come and touch your lovely brother.

Give dear Candriel your flayed and I will return them as instruments of your will.

Come home, sweet beautiful sister, and I will send you back better than ever before.

Suddenly the knowledge was there in her head, always there, merely unlocked now by this her Brother. The way to arrange the bodies as to draw a door, an anchor into her universe, where her new family could help her. Suddenly she felt comfortable.

Willing.

When they drew her out of her dimension she felt no fear, weathered the pain as they opened her skin and drilled their receptors and processors directly to her bones, basked in the soothing lack of anxiety when they twisted her soul, brought out their favorite human qualities—cruelty, greed, corruption, selfishness—and hid her heart from her.

If there was enough of Moray Moon left to wail in agony, wail it would at what it's become.

Borderline were courteous enough to provide Dutch with decent—if a bit outdated—structural diagrams of the under-platform atmospheric mining spike. He's overlaid this on the glasses dimly so he can focus and unfocus his eyes without distraction. The mess hall, living quarters, and workshops are all on the uppermost level. Further down the shaft would be protruding monitor outposts, various setups to draw pure aglaotinum from the planet's ozone and begin its refining process, and at the bottom the main gas dredge and projection dish with featured hangar bay for manned excursions into the maw.

Schultz drops through the aging ventilation into the middle of the old mess hall.

A Necromatic in standby mode is facing the wall opposite. At the clatter of his boots the machine goes into activation, black smoke whirling up from the chest in a rattling clatter of accelerating gears. There's a distant howling as others in the vicinity pick up the signal.

The most recognizable and common of the Kindred's abominations, Necromatics come in several models—Alphas are ex-human. Different designations usually denote construction from the dead of a different species. Corpses so received are fitted over metal endoskeletons bolted to the rotting skin. Terrible weapons are wired to the core. Then the captive soul of the dead, by then corrupted into its basic human instincts—rage, cruelty, greed—is replanted inside the reactor of the machine. The result is a sort of undead demon cyborg, a malevolent and primitive killer draped in the flesh of the person it once was.

Dutch Schultz hates Necromatics almost as much as he hates the Tubal-Cains themselves.

This one looks like a slipshod job—the orifices of the decomposing face haven't even been lined up with those of the alien skull beneath, tufts of frayed wire jutting out of the rot, loops of cable emerging from sores to connect to the bare metal beneath the tissue. The right arm bears a kluge of cogs and gyros that terminate in lawnmower-esque spinning blades. With a crude remoteness the lopsided mouth stretches in mockery of a smile as it prepares to charge.

He's got those wicked bullets for a reason.

Faster than the eye can see the Colt is out, hot silver thunder twice into the chest reactor of the Necromatic and it hits the floor with an ear-splitting shriek, smoke and oil and black blood gushing from the joints.

"Is that you, Schultz?" it moans in cold layers. "Let me fuck you, oh *please*."

He puts another bullet through the laughing black-eyed face. The blueprint says a custodial closet around the hallway's curve is situated above a bathroom one level down. It's more or less guaranteed the structure of the mine spike has changed since the blueprint's publication—application of verticality seems as practical as anything to ascertain Moray's location.

Another Necromatic vaults from the closet, flesh hanging in tattered ropes, roars in Schultz's face as it levels the exhaust-leaking gunbarrel that is its mouth—he puts a bullet through that, one in the chest for good measure, drags the one-ton corpse into the hall.

Then he's stomping on the broom closet's floor like a kid having a tantrum.

He jacks the rotor-tendons in his shins and brings his knees to his chest, slamming down with as much force as he can muster. The crumbling tile beneath caves inwards. Schultz smashes through the drop ceiling, rusted metal, and rotten insulation into an antique porcelain toilet, twists his ankle, shakes to his feet with a snort.

An Alpha roars in and he puts a slug into the reactor, paints the opposite wall black as he moves into the hall. A Necromatic crouched beneath an awning of rib cages stuck to the ceiling launches forward and he grabs the face with his off hand, overamplifies the neuromusculature of his fingers and closes it like he's denting a soup can, crushes the front of the skull to shuddering black pulp. He shakes off alien sludge as the body drops and slides the empty magazine out of the Colt.

Another Necromatic with gunbarrel arms drops down from the decrepit ventilation. Schultz throws a slug through its head but not before it gets a smoking musket-like blast off, a howling black ribbon of solid mist searing the flesh off Schultz's left shoulder by the collar bone. The machine gurgles and moans sensually as Dutch clamps one hand on the wound, pressing hard as the combat skin whispers in his head, "*Warning: coagulation process engaged. Extradimensional carcinogens detected. Please avoid further hazards until a thorough medical evaluation can be obtained.*"

"Why don't you get down and *fuck* me?" The Necromatic runs one dented gunbarrel over its melted crotch and Dutch executes it with the underside of his boot.

The bare abrasion is developing an aching alcoholic burn. He heads through the door at the end of the hall, this room on the map a small bay for weather drones. In reality, it seems to be a storeroom of some sort for Moray, human leather tanning against the walls, old weather probes no more than a pile of junk in the corner with their release doors sealed by rotten skin. A clatter at the end of the room and what looks like it was once a woman is flipping him the bird as she leaps into an open vent.

Dutch pounds after her but can't really fit too well. He ramps his modified tendons and begins to drag himself through, battered and dented boxes of sheet metal falling from under his legs as he smashes down between walls. Bursting out into an old shower room in a hail of plaster, metal, and wet tissue, he shakes dust from his hair and looks up.

"Oh."

Six Alpha Necromatics have scorched gunbarrels trained on him. Gears churn, blades swoosh, the air filling with black exhaust and the sweet reek of decaying flesh as they power up to full with a warbling hum. Behind them Moray disappears down a pipe-lined passageway.

Look, Ma, a target-rich environment.

The burning itch in Schultz's arm diminishes as his combat skin finishes coagulation and arrests the infection and

Have to be very cautious cannot afford you motherfuckers

the glasses are trying to help target

        all   of   at

      once   them   looks from

             he unfocuses

            his eyes   the floor, sees six

confident

        horrors weapons bared with

           bodies

   rotting   off their ill-fitting skeletons

       I FUCKING

Shrieking bolts   leaving the   barrels of their parent weapons

      blazing   tongues   of shadowed night

       Dutch Schultz   twists

his

      torso and   PUTS

      HATE YOU

THEM

    DOWN   one immediate left   POW

one immediate right

behind   shell

     that   cabinet and again   here   casings

another grab its   face and

rolls

        in the   BOOM

cheek at point blank   skin just blows away

  ah right   under that

              table   *MOTHERFUCKING*

clattering   rolls again

       one with a glowing red visor

             behind that chest   that's

   LOCUSTS   four oh the

other two are   BLAM

           coming and one

    say goodbye

The vestigial processing of at least one Necromatic notes before expiring it's never seen anything move that fast.

Schultz stands and drops the second magazine into an empty pouch, primes his third. Pounding down the hall of hissing pipes he pushes his glasses up the bridge of his nose with one finger and focuses anew. There should be a service elevator in the general vicinity that'll take him right near the base hangar.

When Dutch enters the monitoring anteroom he's met with the sight of something that starts a tic under his left eye. Any remaining pain in his shoulder is forgotten. His glasses begin screaming so much data—

WARNING ALERT CAUTION DARK INTENT DETECTED VACATE VACINITY UNKNOWN TOXIC EXTRADIMENSIONAL RADIATION ENTITY LINK DETECTED SUPERSTRUCTURE AT RISK OF VIOLATION BY UNKKNOOWWNWNWNJIIPRRRRAAISISISSSEE THE SHADOWS BEHIND THE STARS WE'LL EAT YOUR HOLES BLOODY WE'LL FUCK YOU RAW

—that he shuts them off entirely.

Moray Moon is crouched atop a bank of dead computer towers,

black eyes shining. Beside her stands a Necromatic that is absolutely not an Alpha model. Schultz's teeth grit as he begins to sweat.

His heart-rate shoots up, fists clenching, eyes rolling.

"Where did you get *that* affront to reality, you senseless cunt?"

It's the Necromatic that answers with an orgasmic groan, turning to face Schultz in full, the orifices near its head oozing and seductive, "*Stuff my fuck-holes, Schultz, fill me up good!*"

"Shut the fuck up!"

Moray laughs as the Necromatic lurches forward on four pincered legs, turreted torso bellowing black smoke. A deep and unintelligible whispering claws at the very edge of Schultz's hearing. The primary receptor looks like the skinned head of a goat or horse, a crooked antenna jutting from one suppurating eye socket, but it's the only recognizable part. Twitching vestigial limbs curl in on themselves from the main bulk, a diseased and contorted pillar bristling with sores birthing arms both metal and flesh bearing weapons, syringes, blades, saws, gun barrels. Sick crimson light glows from somewhere inside, burning out the tattered rotted holes in the skin.

He brings the Colt to bear as Moray rolls away towards a pair of elevator doors.

Twisting backward instead he falls behind a stack of plastic crates as he fires, blasting a hole through her chest as howling black bolts rip through the air where he stood.

Dutch pushes himself prone against a tower of computer banks, sends two silver slugs thundering into the base of the Necromatic's sludgy torso. Dark bronzed metal shears off with flesh in chunks and the thing falls squealing mechanically in several voices at once, firing from its guns wailing gobs of energy so black they suck light from the room and pound misting craters into the walls. Blades scrabble madly, digging sizzling furrows into the floor.

Darting forward Schultz grabs the silver bolo from its sheath with his off hand and buries it into the seizing Necromatic's back, drags down and tears open the decay. Inside its abominable corpse churn the alien machines of the Tubal-Cains. Placing his pistol against the shell of the demon reactor he sends two slugs home, shattering the metal in a hail of rotting matter and gleaming splinters, the unholy glow leaving its eyes.

The room is silent as he catches his breath and approaches Moon, checks her pulse.

There, but barely.

Schultz raises her to a sitting position. The bullet he gave her made a hole the size of a fist coming out of her stomach and she's unconscious from silver shock. He notices her facial features are warped too large for her head, which accompanied with her humped shoulders and the lines of wires running beneath her skin gives her an uncanny puppet-like appearance. He slaps her face a few times but she never comes around.

Still propping her against his arm, he waits for the death rattle.

Acting quickly he opens a pouch near his left hip and pulls out a rusty railroad nail, a little black saucer with a blinking red light attached to the head feeding a wire down near the spike. He twists the head until it whines and then jams it into her throat with a muddy red spurt.

Black eyes bolt open as she tries to scream.

She scrapes at the nail, scrapes at Dutch's face. Fat bloody tears roll from the corners of her rupturing sockets and she gasps before choking out in a voice like an electrolarynx, "They...s-said you... you'd come."

"I'm sure they did, you fucking idiot." His voice trembles with poorly-controlled anger. "How's that deal working out now?"

"Said I'd...be better..."

"Who did? Adrujiel, Sister of Tumors? Candriel, Brother of Decay? Shipped your buddies back over in a gunship, did they, little gift for a number one fan?"

His eyes and lips narrow to barely-visibly slits. "*It's a fucking game,* testing new toys on the Foreman's crew. Doesn't matter if the misery comes from you or me, long as they get it."

She gasps like a dying fish. "I was better...my Family saw..."

"No, you just *think* you're better." He leans in close. "There is *one* human being left in this forsaken fucking universe deserving of it and it is *me* and I will kill *anyone* and *everyone* to keep the Kindred from my home, if that's what it takes. You can take that with you."

Dutch reactivates his glasses.

They've reset:

Contract 409: Moray Moon—Humanoid, Ordovan, Kindred of Tubal-Cain Tech Detected in Bloodstream—On Unauthorized Loan From Sheol Central Processing

The dead never put up much of a fight, obsessed though they are with order, meaning his unauthorized use of a single soul should go unpunished.

Certainly use of one so warped it's barely recognizable.

Moray hacks up a black bloody rope. Another deadbeat criminal turned into an existential threat by the Tubal-Cains. If they can still taste her they'll feel her slip away, though he knows they'd enjoy it, the fuckers.

"Moray Moon, by authorization of the Foreman via contract seal number four-oh-nine, I release you from the burden of your life."

He snaps her neck and rips the railroad nail from her throat in a final arterial gush.

He pulls out one of his directional party-poppers. These are fougasse-like grenades so stuffed with micromunitions they can clear a roomful of assholes in under a second. Setting it against the broken Necromatic he drags Moray's corpse into the service elevator. It begins its descent as a muffled *whump* shakes the structure.

Schultz thought of just squeezing her head off, but since it's in good condition, there's no reason to damage it recklessly. Instead he pulls the bolo and jams it into the hole the spike made, saws around until the head comes loose, the mystic blade cauterizing the cut. He twists and bends the spinal column like a stubborn branch until it breaks.

The elevator shudders to a halt, doors bleating open.

Moray's head held by the hair in his left hand, the Colt in his right, Schultz exits.

There's no sound. In fact there isn't anything. An empty room, the panels falling off the walls and weeping with great streaks of rust. There are holes in the floor where something may have once fit, stains where brackets were removed after years of use, but nothing now. A massive sliding door twelve feet opposite the elevator stands flaking with rust, a trefoil painted over it in something long since gone grey, flanked by a three button panel: "OPEN", "CLOSE", "VENT". An amber hazard light hangs overhead. When Dutch punches the control, the amber light begins to whirl, a dead alarm buzzing at whisper's volume as the door quivers open.

A balcony three feet out and five wide over nothing, a gap, a massive abyss that makes Schultz's chest heave with vertigo. No way of telling if it ends somewhere or just opens right into the Ordovan sky. There is no light. Dutch can just barely see decayed tile making a dome-shape, curving away until the glow from the little room and its amber light aren't strong enough to show the far side.

Schultz lifts Moray's head up. "Is this where you kept the gunship?"

He makes it nod.

"I thought so."

Whipping out a penlight, he flashes the dark below. At first he can't see anything, but after squinting for a moment, he sees that he's panning light across some heaving expanse.

Some mass below is respiring.

The glow passes over ancient gaping sores and then alights on an enormous black-sclera eye, blood-colored iris bulging as the pupil contracts.

It blinks.

Nictitating membrane.

Reeling backwards, Dutch estimates the eye must be the size of a house, given the distance.

Turning off the penlight, he primes and tosses his other party-popper.

He'll wake sweating in a week's time from the sound the gunship makes as it begins to burn, the electric alien bellow of a dying mechanical whale.

Nor will he forget the hundred-foot arm of decomposing flesh that reaches from the flickering flames to grope at the balcony.

Schultz recoils, almost slaps VENT before CLOSE, catches and reverses.

With the muffled sound of automated alarms, the hangar doors open and drop the wailing torched corpse of the Tubal-Cain gunship into the stormy lower night of Ordovan.

Boarding the elevator once more, he lifts Moray's head and looks into its vacant eyes.

"Somebody wants to see you."

TRACKING

Forty minutes out of Deimos and Tracker Barca has the target's scent as we rocket up through the marshes.

Cold rum cake for breakfast—ain't a bad morning, hallelujah.

You take an average panel truck cab V10 under her skirt and no box on the back and she makes a runner like you wouldn't believe. Nailed on some aftermarket metal of our own—road call, motor gangs on the run with the village medicine, corporate agent making waves? Not a problem, lead candy here for all God's children, just a handful of eagles in return.

The reedy marshes are heavily toxic, even mildly radioactive in certain areas so we keep to the berms following a succession of territorial road signs, red stars and black anvils and curve warnings. I do the driving since Tracker Barca has no eyes what with being a Tracker, infra-sonics like boombox speakers jammed into his sockets. Today they're shadowed by a dirty Panama hat. A damp wrinkled cigarette dangles from one corner of his mouth, fingers playing idly with a pearl-handled stiletto. He relights the incense cone on the dash and smiles at me through a gravelly puddle of rotten teeth.

"Balm for your Employment Avoidance Syndrome."

Sure, bluebacks laid on thick.

I'm no angel and I gotta eat.

The marketeers of Deimos pay very little for courier runs these days, sipping pink milk from ornamental glasses and conducting abruptly focused business. The shutters of the Postmen are long locked and bolted, lights gone dark, hang up your goggles. This House of Dog hunting shit is okay because it pays, but goddamn if it doesn't make me nervous as fuck working with Trackers. Morbid fear of abhuman sociopaths I guess.

"She's on foot in Stilton, only basic armaments. Should be able to subdue her. Your iron barks?"

I nod. He's talking about my "wheelman's friend", the hammerless over-under coach gun I'll use to disable her so we can toss her back to the Ottomans. Got a fistful of ten-gauge electromagnetic slugs to do the job. I also strapped a hunting knife to my thigh because it's supposed to be simple but I have this black "looming shitshow" knot in my stomach.

Barca seems like he might feel the same, nailing me with random bits of non sequitur conversation. Very unlike him. I can tell he's eager to get his reputation up in the listings, making nervous idle talk, taking a hardcore red job like this. He returned dark-browed from House of Dog's nerve center.

The Tracker takes out a palm-sized glossy black platelet and projects a flickering blue hologram of the contract dossier from its concave belly. He runs over it out loud a third time as the reeds whisk by hugging bent and beaten girders, wafting through the thick stagnant odor of the marshes.

Bounty: "Jacinta", a YTI Hyacinth-5 Technic Disruptor. One of the old AMIs, Anti-Mechanized Infantry, an anti-tank cyborg sold to a holding company front in Istanbul. She disappears from their roster post-War and starts turning up from New Samarkand to Jakarta, pulling terrorist demolitions and freelance sabotage. Now she's been sighted near Deimos and the Neon and our neck of waste, hiding in the local shanty-towns and market cadres, no doubt looking for her next score, whatever that may be.

The Turkish company's secondary consultant threw down a contract promising a handsome slice of kale for her flowery bodice, and whether hydraulically amplified or not, we do intend to deliver said bodice and earn our keep. We've been warned to keep aware of optic positron discharge and amplified iridium musculature. I'm not super familiar with positron anything except the atomic handguns of the Axis—if she's got anything like that we gotta be real goddamn careful.

Amplified musculature don't sound too fun either.

Radioactive marshes burble a yellow farewell as we pass up and into Stilton, a maze of rickety corrugated tin-and-plank shanties set on scaffolds above the flood line. Fishy eyes stare from lantern-lit hovels, the inhabitants shying away from the rays of sunlight that fall to their floors. We putter into the thick of town and grind to a halt.

No identifiable locations—grocery, civic, nothing. She could be hiding in any of these stinking warrens, titanium limbs waiting to pound us to shreds, secreted behind a horde of fearful shantyfolk. Perhaps they're working with her, perhaps just abetting. No way to tell from here.

The Tracker slides from the cab like a dead weasel and adjusts his hat, takes the platelet from his shirt pocket. A holographic blue hyacinth with five bright petals fizzles into existence. He stares at the homes from the road, then opens his mouth and gives a foghorn bark with infra-sonic amplification that rolls between the planks kicking up wood dust and chips of ancient paint.

Dark eyes glitter in doorways.

Complete silence.

Nature marches on, cicadas buzzing in the reeds, but none of those eyes speak or show, a salty breeze whistling through the wood.

Tracker Barca gives another echoing bellow and this time a shutter bangs somewhere within the maze—he gives me a slow grin and disappears into town with a beckoning hand.

We pass oddly disturbing little scenes, some erased from memory—narrow people with massive eyes eating things that ought not be eaten. Even in the red glare of mid-day sunlight their homes fall to shadow, lit from within by lanterns whispering soft blue light. Dusky cobalt glints off the barrel of a shotgun propped in a corner against pallets and straw. A child wearing a filthy pillowcase eats an orange dusted with red pepper, an adult's hand on their shoulder, their body hidden in the dark. Someone plays cat's cradle with a nest of rusty wire, coils flaking and creaking in their bony fingers.

Every so often Barca will stop me with one hand and lean over to sniff the frame of a door, to run his fingers along depressions in the wooden duckboard, to taste a drop of something yellowish that's soaked into the grain. He fans his face with the Panama hat. I can hear him murmuring to himself, his infra-sonics chuckling back.

"Should've brought shift-traps, maybe some electric snacks..."

A seven-foot woman vaults from a window to Barca's left—he ducks and she smashes overhead through a door to his right, already back on her feet as I bring the coach gun up to my chest. She launches a fist like a cinderblock at the side of Barca's head as he backpedals recoiling, stumbling, vomiting distorted blasts from his infra-sonics that tear the wood of the house behind her to splinter and dust. She staggers, eyes glaring violet, and a screaming spear of light blazes Tracker's left arm from his shoulder as he turns for cover.

She's in my face in a blink, grabs the gun and slams it up and into my face, shattering my nose into a bloody mass – I crumple with the cauterized flesh of Barca's stump in my face. Jacinta grabs his leg and drags him groaning behind her into another house. I scrabble from the duckboards and brass check the coach, lean into the house at a run.

The Tracker kicks at her, grabs at the floor, gets the leg of a wooden chair and begins smashing it into her back. This shatters the chair—she grabs one leg herself and starts wailing on Barca's torso with it. I give her a ten-gauge slug to the chest and she staggers back a moment as the electromagnetics hit, coolant leaking from her shirt. She jerks in place a moment then shakes it off with an accelerating hum, turns and lobs a kerosene lantern that nails the door frame behind me, taking the roof up in a wave of black smoke. Tracker swings at her with his stiletto. She grabs him by the shoulders, headbutts him, slams him through a rickety table.

That's some quality EM shielding.

Gonna have a nice talk with our Turkish consultant about *that* shit.

A charge of shot tears over my shoulder – I turn to see one of the town denizens with a picket-fence grin crouching in the door of the home across the way, reloading a double-barrel of their own. I erase their whole fucking face with a slug like a pulsing steel fist and the townie crumples in a red spray. Behind me Jacinta hurls Tracker by the leg through the ruined wall and into the marshy filth below.

I get my feet under me as she disappears after him.

Priming two fresh cartridges, I lean onto the creaking scaffolding. Little geysers of grey water spray up as splinters scatter and my section of floor gives way into the mud. Jacinta is coming at a prone Barca who's attempting to drag himself free. I see him yell a blast from his sonics that staggers her a moment, try to get to my feet as she spits a rope of yellow coolant. I fire one barrel and then the other into her back before reloading again, blue iron haymakers thudding home in squirts of coolant and she falls face down in the dirt, a red light blinking somewhere out her shrapnel wounds.

Tracker, unsteady on his feet and clutching at his stump, kicks at her ribs. He grins at me, a string of drool from his mouth, and a smooth brown hand reaches up, grabs his shirt and yanks him back into the mud. She brings one hydraulic foot down on his head, which cracks audibly into a bloody slush.

I bolt like fuck to the V10, tear muddy roostertails as I shift into drive.

I'm out of Stilton and good lord I can breathe, my nose is fucking killing me and my boss is dead but I can breathe, now what's on the ol' radio?

In my driver's side mirror I see the flicker of a fluorescent blue hyacinth tattoo as she grabs the back of the cab with arms like piledrivers, keeping pace with the revving truck.

She leaps onto the cab roof.

I yank the e-brake and bring us to a screeching halt in the smell of scorched rubber as Jacinta slams against the hood and onto the road.

I press my foot to the floor and the V10 screams as I scramble for the coach gun.

She rights herself, turns, and *grabs the grill,* digs her feet into the tarmac and—

—*suplexes* my fucking truck.

I shit you not.

I recall the existence of safety belts and slam into the road. The impact should break my neck but doesn't, just the arm I land on as I smash the cab ceiling. My everything begins to hurt, screaming pain and the truck whines pitifully, Jacinta reaching through the shattered window with a skinless metal hand and pulling me back out. Glass tears my arms as I grab for the knife and start hacking weakly at her synthetic flesh. I can smell blood and burning metal and motor oil as I chop and shudder and she holds me aloft by the collar, ribbons of fake skin falling to the ground, dark machine eyes glossy as she bunches up the other hand.

The burning truck radio sputters, "*All our times have come...*"

I'm nearly laughing as she punches through my chest.

THE PARTISAN

The back door is unlocked.

Boomslang peers anxiously up the fire escape, fences to his left and right.

No eyes, human or otherwise.

Up the stairs we go, closed apartment doors on one side blaring the same television channel, apartments on the other with open windows. They're watching the parade floats, flowers and angels and the bright shining sun. Great clouds of pearlescent glitter drift down upon the procession. Boomslang tucks his coat tighter and heads to the top floor, number six. Beneath the coarse cloth metal presses into his skin, lifeless and unyielding.

The last unit before the stairs is watching his favorite movie, *Kentucky Fried Justice*, instead of the parade for some reason, maybe pirate cable. Though time is tight and he knows it he still stops near the door. It sounds like the Inspector is being grilled by the Sebright Brothers; he hears a muffled accent squawk, "What, you think this is a fuckin' yolk? Saunders, show him the gapeworm."

Boomslang laughs quietly.

He'll miss watching that.

The woman stares at him across the rental desk with milky eyes. "So you work *and* live here?"

Boomslang nods. "Yeah, apartment comes with since it's attached. Convenient in the winter."

She smiles. "I bet. I'd go stir crazy, wouldn't be able to detach from work."

Rummaging through her purse she comes out with an embossed card and presents it between two slender fingers. "You give me a ring if you guys get any new product. I'm in the area."

"Yeah, sure."

Comfortably vague:

CATHERINE BURGOS—UTILITY—ALL CONTRACTS

As she walks outside, the woman rubs one eye absentmindedly and a contact falls out. Scrambling on the handicap ramp, Boomslang comes outside to help her and she ducks down, covers her eye with one hand. He sees a glint of sun on plastic and reaches for the clouded lens. Turning away she thanks him and pops the contact in. They shake hands and Burgos heads to her car. When she's out of his sight, a nictitating membrane slides across her eye and glues the contact in place, filmy with moisture.

On the sixth floor of the apartment building Boomslang finds a door marked near the knob with a tiny silver star. Finding it unlocked he enters. Dusty sheets cover armchairs and tallboys. The window's long shattered, shards of glass dusting the sill like rock candy.

He stays away from there.

No need to be seen until he needs to be seen.

He sits in shadow beneath a rafter and pulls metal from under his coat, begins assembling his bow from lengths of fiber-optic cable and old arcade cabinet. Outside the atonal parade music sets his teeth on edge, dissonant chimes the angels claim stimulate healthy brainwave activity. The only stimulation Boomslang can relate from them is the over-stimulating they gave his shell-shocked nervous system, chimes in his head, as they began their attempts to comb out his "undivine thought processes".

Boomslang plans on stimulating *their* nerve endings, if they have any.

Catherine's long legs are shaved smooth as the bedsheets. Boomslang lies on his back between them, resting his head on her breast as they talk about nothing at all. It's warm outside, uncharacteristic for the season. She runs her hands through the tangle of his hair with a sigh.

"Gonna brew some brew, you down?"

She nods. "Half and half, no sugar."

"Cream okay?"

She nods again as he leaves the room, rubbing the brand on the back of his neck. While he busies himself in the kitchenette, she rolls to her crumpled jeans and paws through the pocket palm computer, sends out an auditory code for her superiors – DELINQUENT TARGET MARKED. They'll chatter and fawn over that in their strident language. She turns back over, tosses the tablet onto her clothing, wonders if Boomslang noticed anything at all when she squeezed the organic probe down his urethra, spasming in the throws of pleasure.

When he returns with coffee she smiles, takes the proffered mug, kisses his cheek. "What do you want to do today?"

"I'm going to drink my coffee and watch *KFJ* before I wash the car."

"That fucking movie."

"That movie indeed."

The light-bow is ready. That's his term and a bit fancy – really just a bespoke electron beam projector Boomslang built from junk salvage. It's about as likely to explode in his hands as it is to fire, but he holds faith he can at the very least scar the angel on the final float.

The bottoms of his pantlegs are bloodied from blisters and he changes over to his last clean wrappings, careful to cover the pads of his aching toes. Tipping a plastic flask against his lips he drinks its dregs, wipes his mouth with one dirty coatsleeve as he moves low to the window.

The parade rear is bringing it in, the final float a gilded affair of glowing silver bars and fluorescent white rings, visual distortion from the power of the angels' music. There are no tires beneath— angel technology has it adrift via repulsive generators, steered by the power of extrinsic minds. There's a message blaring from the float that Boomslang can't understand. He's long since removed his own copy of the personal translator implanted within each living human.

Had to marinate the drill tip in alcohol and bite a leather belt, but he did it.

"I want to know what's so goddamn important. A month, without word."

"We aren't married. We have no contract together."

"That a relationship to you? More company work? Got you right back on the palm computer you're fucking glued to anyway?"

"No, it's just—you don't owe me anything either."

"You have to know I care, Cat. It's not a fuckin' surprise." Chewing on his cheek, Boomslang slams the door behind him, knowing it's petty, getting angrier for it.

In the bathroom she stares herself down in the mirror, eyes flickering.

"No contract. No contract. No contract."

Each time a different persona—man, woman, gurgling bestial growl.

Raindrop in a hurricane Boomslang thinks, taking aim through a sight carved from a glass pop bottle. In his home-painted crosshairs, the angel's face, palest flesh nearly translucent pulled tight over the skull, an antler sprouting from the forehead like a sprig of petrified birch. The single eye spins erratically in its socket, focusing and unfocusing too quickly to follow. Boomslang's hands are shaking so badly he puts the bow down, rests them a moment, breathes deeply.

If people see angels take harm, maybe they'll stop trudging around like whipped dogs.

What would the Inspector say?

"Gonna see you cracked and fried, motherclucker."

Doesn't fit.

Boomslang places the bow on the window, his finger tightening around the trigger, and suddenly there's a twisting knot of pain in his testicles so powerful he drops to the floor yelping. Ripping his pants off he gropes for his junk with his free hand. A dull green light blinks from within the skin of his scrotum and he knows she must have put it there, finally gets it.

He's not stupid.

Neither are they.

At the faintest hint of energy discharge, the probe pipes out to the orbiting angel dreadnaught one message. The micro-organic's only job complete. A beam of holy light no wider than an inch pierces through the roof of the apartment building and Boomslang's skull, blows his eyes and his life and his ache out across the dusty wooden floor in a superheated white burst of understanding.

DESERTION

The town of Duskfall has long fulfilled its namesake—shuttered and silent for nigh on fifty years, another habitation lost in the nightmare warren of rejected architecture that litters the Central States Axis, its townspeople long fled.

Something else has taken up residence.

It's alerted by the sudden *WHUMP* of the main gate bursting to splinters via breaching charge. Two figures enter, extremities insulated against weather and harm by the vestments of their profession. One takes what looks like a sliver of metal folded origami-style from a pocket of her uniform; the other coughs up a crimson string that dangles from his chin, steadying himself with the book chained to his waist.

Static breaks the silence anew. "Come in Cabal-One. You reading us, Singh?"

The first, who's also been fiddling with the knobs on a strange-looking tube of machinery, raises a finger to her lips and quietly shushes the other.

"Cabal-One?"

A petite Indian woman, whip-thin with her hair in a bun at

the nape of her neck, Apoorva Singh wears jeans with boots and a black button-up under her dark khaki Axis coat. The coat signifies her Handler status, witching patches on the shoulders and lapels. Her belt pouches are sparse—extra bark for Sobczek, nutrition supplements for herself, the aforementioned tube of machinery. A few wards and tools but Sobczek is the actual shaman.

By chewing the addictive *morto* bark, Cabal Theurgists condemn themselves to a life of rotten teeth, social prejudice, and alien visions of the dead that can reach such an apex of personal fear most witches remove their own eyes, by medicine or by hand. Theurgists are those warlocks who've been hired by the Central States Axis to tap this power for their use, usually hired on with the promise of better care—a promise kept on the shakiest of terms. To this end, trained Handlers are assigned to each witch, provided with aid equipment and sent out as two-person teams, usually with set strikes in mind. Theurgists are for surgical operation. No witch yet has been used in any large-scale war context, to the relief of those who fear their particular retribution.

Sobczek secures his copy of the Book of Shades. This text makes the Cabal what it is. Each Theurgist, in addition to their own varied powers, is taught Rephaic and how to call their fallen forebears from Sheol for aid. For Handlers like Singh, weapons come in the form of machinery like her tube of Toadfire, a mystically-enhanced heat projector using sacred oils wrung from the dead. The name refers to the flame's sickly green tint—a lethally toxic weapon against the deceased.

For witches like Sobczek, the weapons are the dead themselves.

Singh primes the pipe for use with her final vial and sheaths it, the cone adjusted to provide a wide torching angle. The main street of Duskfall presents no current targets.

Slapping the folded slice of metal between her hands it unfurls into a tiny mechanical bat, organic components in the wings and processor maintained by a small circulatory web in the body. Fledermaus are mostly for reconnaissance purposes but can be modified to set shaped explosives or discharge their battery in an atomic blast. Cabal-One's Fledermaus can drill into malleable ground and send out a sonar pulse for immediate target detection.

It works both ways.

"Bat says the Town Hall should have aid for a map projection."

Sobczek scratches absentmindedly at his shadowed cheekbones, the last bit of face exposed before the iron plate that's been drilled into every shaman's cranial bone over their eyes. Little streaks of dried blood and tears stain the sides of his nose. "I don't know what I have left in me."

"I know. Let's keep moving and take it a step at a time, okay?"

The sun is midway through setting beyond a blanket of smoked ivory, earth and town bathed in a baleful glow made surreal by the gritty wind. The steeple-like rooftop of the Town Hall looms overhead. Cabal-One ascend the creaking steps with planked wood bending at their weight.

Behind them, something laughs like a hyena, a maddened pitch that chokes off in the wind. Singh whips her Toadfire around behind them. Nothing immediate—which doesn't change her belief that something might be beyond sight. The chills tell her she ought to keep the projector readied all the same.

The Town Hall is a dead end. The back end has buckled with time and wear, blocking doors and windows with plaster-dusted rubble and beams. The building is silent except for a periodic scuttling, the drip of stagnant water. Both of them jump when Singh's belt yips—the Fledermaus transmitting its current general surveillance route. This is projected holographically out of the machine's back along with a happy little clip art of a smiling bat.

Sobczek stretches, cracking his back. "Fucker nearly gave me a coronary."

Singh holsters the Toadfire and wipes sweat from her forehead. "Any thoughts on that laughter?"

Sobczek shakes his head. "Nothing yet, anyways." He removes the Book of Shades from its cage and unclasps the locks, letting the fetid pages fall open across his hands. Sobczek once admitted to Singh that when he ran his fingers across the words, something with a voice like creaking ice squeezed them into his ear. This prompted Singh to wonder, on her own and in silence of course, if the dead could and would modify their conjury to consider a specific user base.

Sobczek unsheathes his ritual knife and, muttering in Rephaic, slices open one palm, smearing the blood in a circle in the air where it stays as if smudged on glass. He squeezes out a few drops onto the pages of the book. The blood flares white-hot before fading from view.

"Should cover our tracks."

They're on the lam.

Theurgists and their Handlers aren't supposed to fall in love.

Nor are you supposed to use a mission as cover to desert the Axis—but that's obvious.

CSA specialists will already be looking for the bodies of the other Handler-Theurgist pair, probably with Tracker support straight from House of Dog. As for the original intent of the job—it's an Axis issue. They'll be long gone by the time it would ever be their problem.

Singh manipulates the holographic map with shaking fingers. The town is small but walled, one end dominated by a single church. On the sewage-spewing cliff behind them, an abandoned mall sits leaning like the decaying body of some strange titan. Beyond the town is farmland then forest sliding from fertile to fallow to toxic as one travels.

"Babe." Sobczek puts his hand over hers and kisses her fingers when she turns.

"Yes, hello there. With town records in, the Bat'll navigate us till the battery runs out. Lots of local data available," and Singh shuts down the map, sends the Fledermaus fluttering around them. "We can check around for food real quick if you want."

"Do you think we have time?"

Singh thinks on the radio. "Will it have mattered if we starve to death in a few days?"

Sobczek shrugs.

Given the condition of the general store when she peeks through its fogged and broken windows, Singh considers it a dead end as well. She's checking the holomap for any other worthwhile locations when in her peripheral vision she sees Sobczek begin backing towards her. He bumps against her shoulder without turning.

"Kyle?"

"Something's over there."

She turns where he's staring and sees only red dust whipping across the street. "Where?"

He points dead ahead, his finger trembling, and she looks. Again, dust.

"Tell me how to help, Kyle. I can't see anything."

"Holy shit, what the fuck *is* that," he moans, blood-flecked tears running from under his plate.

Singh twists the Fledermaus' middle section once in one direction and twice in another and drops it into the ground, where it burrows in and sends out a nice fat sonar ping. Kyle trips over nothing and hits the ground ass-first. He starts scooting backwards.

"Cold."

The Bat projects holo of the sonar. Singh looks from it to the dust and back again, trying to discern some form or shape.

Sobczek grabs her wrist and she jumps. "Go, let's go, let's go *now*."

He leads her back through a wood-lined alley dense with bare laundry string. The Fledermaus flutters after them, chirping quietly. Singh hears Sobczek begin sobbing as they make a wide circuit around the outside of the town back towards its church. Something about the fact that she can't see whatever Kyle's seeing greatly unsettles her.

They pass the Town Hall.

The door is ajar.

They're about to mount the church steps when without turning Sobczek yells, "Behind us!"

Singh crouches and jabs the pipe over one arm. The Toadfire vomits a four-foot tongue of icy jade flame that blisters her shoulder with cold. She turns to see the fire dissipate harmlessly in the air before Sobczek yanks her into the church. Still calling her name he drags her down a flight of stairs behind the pulpit as something begins shattering the pews to kindling.

At the bottom of the stairs he slams a metal door shut behind them and cranks the vault-like wheel latch shut. Singh raises both shoulders. "What is this?"

"I don't know. I could barely see it below the church. The iron in the door, really."

It looks like some sort of storeroom. They pull the string on the single bare lightbulb. Shelves of canned and boxed foods, jugs of water, a stack of car batteries. A shelter? If so a pre-War one, as everything in the room is covered in a several-centimeter blanket of dust.

In the back of the room, atop an ancient metal desk cluttered with strips and strips and strips of useless crumbling readout, sits a word processor connected to an ancient dot-matrix printer. Neither will turn on, but a terribly faded sheet of paper dangles from the printer's face, as if its dying move were to eject this message.

```
—04:32 in the morning, local time, a——
detected through remote sensors having emerg——
beria. Local units attempted to engage with
standard fi—— ons Procedures Sectio—se 4—"Avto—
— o no avail. Threat engaged local units
identif—pe 9 via method of attack and manner
of behavi—— entrails and disabled th—— rters
has authorized a D66 on last confirmed location.

W        A        R        N        I

Ty—yond malicious—ibited behavior of a nature
sui—— ds for a D66 and requires nothing le——
ll support (see Operations Procedures Section
6—17—— ected Energy— om the necessary units. If
possible—— cene for support as well. Type 9 can
be ba—— of Reve—— Chippewa, Ojibwe, Potawatomi.
```

Beneath this, in chicken scratch, someone's scrawled:

YOU CAN'T SEE IT
BUT IT CAN SEE YOU

Something has begun to pound methodically on the vault door. The
initial strike makes them both jump—each successive hit is stronger
and louder than the last. Individual rivets begin popping onto the
floor. Dents are appearing in the worn iron.

"Kyle?"

"Yes."

She folds the printed paper into her pocket. "We need a way out
of here. Yesterday."

"Right, right." He whips out the Book of Shades, begins palming
through the leaves and filling the air with a musty odor. He rushes
past basic guidance divination and physical incantation to a thin flap
on transit. Beginning to run his fingers across the page Kyle stops.
"You...'Poorva, you know this isn't going to be pleasant."

"Neither is whatever's breaking down the door. Please get us out of here."

He nods, a thin trickle of blood seeping from beneath the plate,
and begins to run his fingers over the text. He reads through the

conjure twice, and then coughs to clear his throat. Every few seconds, the door dents a half inch inward.

Rephaic being the dead language, it tends to sound like one is whispering and inhaling simultaneously during attempts to speak and Singh will never get used to hearing it. As Sobczek communes with Sheol, his eyes begin to bleed from beneath his iron plate. Something begins to softly answer him in inaudible whispers from the pages of the book.

Behind the pounding iron, something yelps a cracked laughter.

Sobczek wipes the blood from his face with the back of his sleeve. "Find me an empty container, please."

Singh tosses him a cardboard box sagging with mildew. Somehow he both catches it and places it on the ground neatly before him with the open side facing upwards. Taking out his ritual knife Sobczek cuts a slice in the palm that's not fresh, smears the sides of the box with half-circles of blood. On the inside bottom he drips a thin oval.

"Can you hold the book?"

The vault wheel on the iron door is dangling off by only a few rivets.

The room has begun to get cold, their breath visible in the dim little shelter.

Sobczek pushes himself away from the box and takes a deep breath. As Singh holds the book up, he runs his hands down the page. He speaks intermittently in Rephaic and English.

"**Boka ma tirichak ro ek tum.**"

Singh looks over to see a rising loaf of veiny skin inside the cardboard box. An incision forms down the middle and bleeds.

"**Shekla beth roet.**"

The skin has risen over the top of the box, leaking blood down the musty sides. From within the slit Rephaic whispering begins to ooze, greasy and hoarse.

"**Te thawem ti ko.**"

The banging on the door gains a sudden bass and Singh looks to see it buckling incredibly slowly, a rivet flying out at a snail's pace to bop off a shelf.

The corpse of a woman wrapped entirely in filthy gauze bandages pulls herself out of the fleshbox. The fabric over her torso is black with blood and as long as she emerges it never seems to become a waist or hips. There's a battered iron mask bearing an Olmec grimace chained around her skull, loose links of metal jangling against her shoulders. Tufts of frayed colorless hair jut from gaps beneath the mask—no face can be seen below. The woman raises a burnt finger with a long yellow nail and moans from beneath the cast in a way that's both bone-chilling and uncomfortably seductive.

Singh closes the book slowly. Kyle coughs. "You see it?"

SCARI TETH KO.

"Please."

IOBEK SEM TAKOL.

"I asked you in the old way. The polite way."

The bandaged woman rocks slowly from side to side, her voice the buzzing of cicadas. **SPARA TU GE KAROTEK.**

"Mother—please."

The woman snaps her neck to him, to Singh. Then she drags them into the slit. Singh's chest seizes up but somehow she slides inside with a wet *schloop*. Before the canal closes, they hear the shelter door give way and a high-pitched giggle like breaking ice.

They fall through neither dark nor light nor hot nor cold but wet and glistening. They rocket through slickness, hands clasped tight, the passage narrowing and then they're on the ground in a pile of dry straw. Somewhere beneath her Singh can hear the croaking moans fading away as if from a great distance, diminishing, then gone. They're laying on the earthen floor of a barn. No living animals are corralled here but in the back a prone horse rots.

Kyle is crying, curled into a ball on the straw pile. Singh kneels down next to him and he opens his hand to show a silver chain, one end charred black, the other broken. "She remembered," he whispers, and then curls further, his chest heaving, breathing labored and wheezy.

Apoorva leaves him there and exits the barn.

Dead fields, a town on the horizon and the suggestion of the mall yet further, a broken windmill creaking ominously. The farmhouse, long since collapsed on one side, the timbers charred black. The Axis Spire long in the distance, barely a shadow against the clouds.

The kitchen.

Blood on the stove.

Oven door ajar.

Black bones in the fireplace.

She activates the Fledermaus when she's standing outside the barn again, the farmhouse crypt leering back from across the drive. The Bat says that they're about fifteen miles west of where they were in Duskfall. Then it unfolds completely into a wide octagon, a format Singh has never seen.

"Fucking *nailed* it!" says the Fledermaus. It's a radio voice, an Axis voice. "Triangulated right in. Retention are on their way and you're now officially in a world of shit. I hope you enjoy being dragged back next to the corpses of your allies you fucking prick." The Bat tears itself into geometric metal pieces in a little spurt of blood.

Then she's grabbing for Kyle, who's kneeling head cocked staring at the back wall of the barn, palms tacky with pus. He mutters something to himself as she approaches.

"Come on baby, we gotta move. They found us."

He clenches the chain to his chest. "Already?"

"It was the Bat. I should have guessed. I'm sorry."

He's shaking his head. "Fuck right okay, uh, let's go. Where are we?"

"She left us at some farm fifteen miles from Duskfall."

"A farm?"

"Sure looks like it. Let's go."

They're not far down the road when aerial whistles portend the gunmetal capsule that smashes into the ground before them. Slats in the side vomit cold mist and then four soldiers in full black-and-tan Axis Retrieval combat armor. Goggled eyes bead positron pistols on the Handler and her Theurgist.

"Get on the ground! Get on the fucking ground!"

Sobczek raises his bloodied hands and simply falls over. Singh goes to grab him—one of the soldiers shoots the ground next to them. She cradles Kyle up. "Fuck you, man."

The soldier speaks into his wrist. "Get your ugly ass down here. We've got 'em." Then he turns to look down at them. "I should fucking spit -" and then he's dragged into the air and becomes frostbitten, his lips and mouth beneath the goggles turning stark white and then black as with a dry suffocating sound he dangles.

The other soldiers aim up, not sure what to fire at or where. One by one each is frozen in place and drained with sockets and jaws agape. Singh isn't sure what to do at all except gather Sobczek up, as he seems to have shut down, try to get back to the farmhouse. A hundred feet away, beside them as they run, something unseen bursts through the walls of the barn in a blast of splinter and planks.

"Kyle *what is that* Jesus *fuck!*"

He remains silent, breathing shallow. She bolts through the front door of the house, looking for somewhere to hide. Outside, a fat black armored car screeches to a halt in the dust. As she pounds up the decrepit staircase and across the remains of the upper floor, she checks the windows. The two soldiers who exit the van are met with the sight of their comrades dead of violent frostbite and hung from nothing. They begin to gesticulate in confused fear.

"Put me down," mutters Sobczek.

"Huh?"

"Put me down."

"Babe, they're not—"

"Please." There's such a painful tone that she places him on the rotting floor by big peeling loops of yellow wallpaper where he moves to a kneeling position. Downstairs, something gives a throaty chuckle.

"Get out of here. If we both die then it was all such a waste." He takes the last of the morto from her belt pouch and stuffs it into his mouth, chewing greedily, and snatches the Toadfire from its holster.

"I love you, Apoorva. Get the fuck out of here!"

"I love you! Kyle, what *is* this thing?"

He laughs and she hears that he's terrified into insanity. Singh turns and drops down from a tongue of splintered wood, tears falling from her eyes.

The soldiers are staring agape behind her, paying no attention whatsoever to her approach. From this angle one can only see the front of the house. A laugh, an insane piercing cackle, the windows bursting with a scream of excruciating agony. The farmhouse explodes with green flame from within.

Singh drops to her knees.

One of the soldiers ditches his gun and bolts.

The other runs to where she's rocking and sobbing. *"What was that? What the fuck was that?"*

She can only rock and sob.

A month later, in an Axis cell, she seems him one night post-gruel.

His face slides from the shadows beneath her only window, opposite the bars.

Somewhere down the arched stone hall a door slams.

It's Kyle but the plate is gone – the bare and tender flesh of his face is exposed and seems to be suffering from advanced frostbite. His teeth are wet yellow tombstones rotting in a mouth strangely twisted, stretched, as if erased and drawn back on too big. The greatest horror may be the enormous glossy black fish eyes, too big for the face and neither the same size, that roll in his deformed once-empty sockets.

"It's the smell, Apoorva."

She brings her knees to her chest, rocks on the bare cot.

It's not you it's not you it's not you

"But it smells like him in here. Inside."

Crocodile tears are rolling down her cheeks and she covers her head but it comes through, that horrible inhuman voice, like a squealing pick to the eardrum.

"I'll finish the rest and then...and *then*..." Giving another batshit little giggle, the jaw distends like a snake's to show the raw stump of its tongue as the face disappears back into the shadows. Apoorva begins screaming and doesn't stop until they come to sedate her. The little voice skates sing-song across the mad ice of her mind, "*Locked in your cell, no one to tell...*"

COBRA ROJA

Victoria hops the Zebulon 88's caboose out of Puerto Amarillo on its way toward Saragossa and points southerly.

Her ticket's not paper—rather her ability to grab the car's handle before the train's going fast enough to dislocate her shoulder, but after it's gained enough speed that intrepid onlookers won't arrest her leap.

She manages the jump and swings on against the back of the caboose. A station attendant runs to the end of the platform waving a fist in the air. She flips a cheery bird.

From one pocket she pulls a WANTED poster. This sucker was tacked to the stationmaster's office, bears her likeness and the words "COBRA ROJA—DANGEROUS HIGHWAYWOMAN—REWARD $10,000". It flutters in the train's wake before floating off to disintegrate on the charred desert floor.

Now she need only reach Saragossa and La Hija de la Noche—from there she'll hopefully find the way to the Black Meridian, from there the great Presidio de Calavera. Within that nebulous prison remains her elder half-sister Lupe, whose cell number sits carved into the flesh of Victoria's underarm where she scarred it the night of her escape.

66A-B6N.

In a tattered campaign coat and pants plated at the joints and shoulders with battered iron, dark buckled knee-high boots and elbow-length fingerless gloves, her grackle's-throat hair pulled back and tied against her skull, Victoria looks every bit the DANGEROUS HIGHWAYWOMAN she is. It's been half a decade since she fled the Presidio herself, five long hard goddamn years of running, robbing, and stabbing—the Plague Year one of them.

Five too soon she returns to the cavernous shadow of Warden de Silva.

She sidles quietly through the caboose and glances into the window of the rear car door.

Women in bustle dresses with floral hats perched atop peaked hair, gentlemen in bowlers and pork-pies with ties tightly knotted, champagne flutes, plates no bigger than one's palm bearing crustless sandwiches, laughter, the quiet internal hum of the train.

Then she spots it.

Halfway down the car, seated facing Victoria, a man-shape in a wide-brimmed hat and clerical collar with stole and pectoral cross. Its head is lowered towards its intertwined hands. It's far and away a foot taller than anyone else in the train, and as if it knows she's looking in, it raises its face and stares with pitch-colored eyes from behind a bone-white tragedy mask.

She ducks back down.

A Predicant.

A hunter of the prison, skip tracer of the destitute.

The Predicant stands, spreads its arms wide, beseeches the travelers around it with a voice somehow as gravelly as it's resonant. "Good children of the Lord! Though it irks me to defile your merry-making, I fear the terrible criminal Red Snake now befouls this conveyance. Hurry along the train to safety, if it please you!"

There's murmuring, some smattered chuckles. A man's voice— *"Está seguro de eso, Padre?"*

"If it's the providence of the Lord you doubt, I urge you—open the door of this car and look for yourself."

Further murmuring.

"I thought not."

Any noise peters out ahead and Victoria inhales deep, realizes they're filing into the next car.

"Come out, Victoria."

She comes running, dagger held in the fencer's grip. The Predicant catches her first swipe by the wrist, twists and flips her to floor. She kicks herself back up just as one slablike fist dents the car floor with an echoing *CLANG*. The Predicant comes swinging – she jukes to the middle aisle and it obliterates a row of ornate seats in a cloud of splinters and down.

"Accept ye God's judgment!"

It comes back at her. Victoria aims a kick at its crotch and is rewarded with a shock of pain reverberating up her leg. The Predicant laughs. She vaults back up and slips her dagger in between the preacher's face and its mask, digs in with effort and pries the facade to the floor where it shatters as it tosses her from itself like a ragdoll.

"*Blasphemer,*" it whispers, the bloodless decay beneath the mask like melting wax, ancient staples come undone. The flesh sloughs away entirely revealing an assymetric jumble of uncanny machinery. Black eyes flicker—the mechanism splits in three and Victoria hurls herself away at the wall as a beam of white light divides the train car laterally, the Predicant swinging its weaponized head in a maddened attempt to cleave her asunder. The car ahead peels apart in a gush of molten metal and spews screaming dismembered nobility to the desert floor amid a volley of cauterized limbs.

Launching first the knife Victoria bolts forwards, the dagger striking the horrid cogs of the Predicant's head a half-second before she grabs and twists it deep, blade breaking off at the hilt, the preacher-thing falling to the floor twitching and shrieking as chunks of metal and runners of oil spatter the decimated car's splintered wooden floor.

The train remains in motion as she works her way through the ruins, worn trucks trundling along with a clatter that hints they're close to detaching. The coaches ahead contain the frightened and crying passengers who remain, heads bowed, finery dirtied with fear, peering disrobed from sleeper compartments with hollow eyes. The dining car is the scene of a culinary massacre, lobster thermidor and butternut bisque covering the windows where servers and diners panicked at the sudden violence.

In the streamlined engine the engineer catches zees draped over his chair with one hand clasping a massive pair of headphones to his ears, oblivious to the recent upheaval and the flashing lights that indicate it. Victoria, quantities of blood and oil splashed upon her clothing, taps him on the shoulder. He throws his head awake with an exasperated sigh.

"*Dios mío*, not again."

"I want to be in Saragossa by nightfall. What're you gonna do about it?"

"This is cruising speed, *amiga*. I can jam her higher but it'll crack the pistons."

"Let's do it."

Stepping neatly to the door, he doffs his hat. "She's all yours, *Capitán*," he lisps, and walks briskly from the train at a cool eighty knots, disappearing into the desert.

Fumbling with the controls, Victoria detaches the remaining cars from the train and pushes a prominent lever to its apex, the engine launching forward across the mesa-strewn landscape with red-powder roostertails flung behind.

Sometime before sunset, the engine car of the Zebulon 88 comes coasting into Saragossa Station like a gunmetal ghost and smashes into the stopblock, not a soul on board or a car in tow, three of the engine's dozen pistons blown out and smoking black.

Victoria enters Saragossa's city limits by foot via the orbiting slums under a faded orange sky.

She dreamt of visiting as a child. As an adult, she's been three times, twice in a jailer's carriage, and the dream is no more.

She walks a maze of corrugated tin and rotting planks, looking for the telltale paintings that lead to her mark. Casting its shadow across the east is La Gran Catedral de Saragossa, effectively marking the entire city enemy territory. With proximity to the church comes Predicant presence, enemy territory.

Luckily she needn't get much closer.

She finds the painted moon of skulls on the faded brick of an old mill, follows it to a brother on the underside of an abandoned cafe awning.

One inside of an overturned dustbin.

A Predicant, three armored young deacons trailing, appears

at the end of a slum row. Victoria ducks into a threshold as they approach, platemail clanking. In the darkened room behind her she can hear the wet smacking sounds of someone chewing with their mouth open.

The church patrol is close—she can hear the Predicant's soft rumbling.

The chewing sound approaches.

They pass outside—their backs to her, they move further down the alley.

The chewing is close and now something worse, a soft guttural chuckle, somehow animal. The retinue turns out of sight at row's end and Victoria flees her hiding spot in the opposite direction, eyes peeled for painted symbols. Did cold fingers brush her collar as she left the threshold? She thinks they might've, but can't be certain.

The next moon of skulls is painted over a manhole cover.

The last in miniscule at the crumbling foundation beside a nondescript tenement.

The woman who answers Victoria's knock is younger than she expected by about forty years, clothed in a linen dress and worn wooden sandals. Charms and bones hang from her wrists and neck, are tethered up in her clay-dreaded locks. She gives Victoria an appraising glance. "*Me encontraste.*"

Victoria's not exactly surprised, but it's still disconcerting. "I'm looking for a road."

"Dark enough I was unable to see it ahead of time, *sin que tu misma estuvíeses aquí.* Come in, and be quick. *La misa va a empezar.*" She bars the door behind them.

The inside of the Daughter's home is a single room lit by a pair of oil lanterns facing each other on opposite walls. The rearmost corner is a functional kitchen. The stone floor is bare but for thin mats of reed; the walls are adorned with scrolls of papyrus and canvas in an alphabet Victoria knows and several she doesn't. A single low table sits dead center surrounded by cushions – on it is a flintlock pistol, a shallow brass bowl, a teapot. A small painted wagon wheel rests beside. A thurible above pumps out dark clouds of incense that make her head spin.

"*Sentar.*"

She does, legs crossed beneath her, as the Daughter walks to the back wall and returns with a steaming bowl of thick-looking champurrado.

"*Beber.*"

Victoria does so, rivulets of chocolate cutting through the ash on her face, the warmth of it spreading along her travel-weary limbs. La Hija pours them sweet, cold black tea in tin cups. These they drink in silence, the Daughter never taking her eyes from Victoria's.

"*Años de sangre.* What road could *you* be looking for? You've sat beside a hundred others, cutting the purses off those who travel them."

"To the Black Meridian and the fortress of the skull. My sister—"

The Daughter waves a hand. "Stupid idea, but fine. *Primero esperamos.*" She takes the flintlock pistol in her hand and crosses her arms.

"We wait?"

The bruja puts a finger to her lips.

An hour later without once having moved, as Victoria's getting truly drowsy, the Daughter fires the pistol—in the darkened room, barely the wind nor public audible outside, the sound is deafening.

"I think I just pissed myself."

La Hija walks over to the back corner of the hovel and returns with the corpse of a bloated rat, a single ragged hole through its middle. She opens it with the edge of the flint pan and dumps the rat's steaming entrails into the brass bowl, moves them around a bit with the barrel. Adding the pistol ball and used powder, she mashes the mess together with her hands in a foul paste and slathers it along the outer rim of the wagon wheel. She leans forward with one slender finger covered in blood.

Victoria grabs her wrist. "What are you doing?"

"You want your road or not?"

Released, she paints Victoria's cheeks, nostrils, the curve of her lips with streaks of rat's blood.

"Wedge the wheel between your palms."

The Daughter spins the wheel. Victoria expects it to bunch the skin of her hands and tear them raw but instead it seems as if she weren't there, as if it's gliding down a road all its own. The Daughter puts a lit pipe in Victoria's mouth, watches as she inhales and takes it for herself.

The spokes begin to blur. La Hija de la Noche swallows the pistol ball and falls unconscious, the pipe forgotten.

Spinning.

Spinning.

A white plate, spinning.

The hulls of rusted ships rotting against the scrubbed desert floor.

Cracked pavement and sputtering electric light.

A man on a floor, a woman in a room, candles and blood, a dying mollusc.

Victoria jolts forward with a start, groggy with the sleep of hours, as La Hija sits up with a gasping inhale and vomits the pistol ball out in a thin gruel. Panting, she wheezes, "*Hacia el sur, hacia las carrteras muertas,* land of dying seas. Under the New Moon, a bank of smoke up the steps of the shrine. *No regresarás.*"

"Who told you? What did you see?"

"You're not supposed to ask."

"How do I know you're not lying?"

"You came all this way to ask a well-known liar?"

Night has long since set.

She pours them cups of tea with shaking hands. "New moon's in two nights. Inns down the road. One with the turtle has your wanted poster up somewhere, one with the tits on it's clear. Rooms on the second floor. Good luck. *Vete.*"

A hot midnight shower at the Lusty Strumpet Inn and Victoria's crashed in her undergarments on the threadbare cot, a torsion grip in her right hand, her lips and face clean of rat.

The shy bargirl who checked her room was blushing too hard to examine her closely; the patrons, too drunk to notice. She's grateful. It's nice up here with the inn's proprietary copper water pitcher and down blanket, the kerosene lamp and shuttered window.

In the night's silence the gears begin to turn, old thoughts cycling as often they do.

Did Lupe think she was dead? Did she feel abandoned the night Victoria kissed her fingers through the bars of her door before fleeing that terrible edifice? Would she forgive her for leaving, for the terrible things she did to stay focused, stay moving, stay alive in the interim? For the lives she took during the Plague Year, her fever-maddened mind obsessed with prolonging her own?

She lifts her right arm to look at Lupe's cell number, carved into the soft flesh of the fore with a broken nail, though she's stared so much over the past five years she knows it from memory.

66A-B6N.

Was Lupe dead already? Tortured out of suspicion she knew Victoria's plan?

Wraith thoughts haunt her mind for years and from years, fear and anxiety high-octane and unleaded, a neurotic nitrous driving her forward, back to the prison, back to Lupe. Upon formulating her departure and making it happen, she could think only of surviving long enough to come back prepared. She never considered the myriad miscommunications, the physical harm her lack of big-picture foresight might have brought until she had already left, was on her way back to the land of the sun. Too little too late, twenty-twenty hindsight, thoughts reactive instead of proactive.

Outside, a Predicant can be heard making a clanking patrol through the slums, searching for rogues and heretics to crucify along the outer wall.

In the humid night air of the inn Victoria falls into a restless sleep.

Next afternoon the bargirl, flushed candy-apple red, tops Victoria's canteen and passes along a sackcloth bag.

"W-Where you headed?" she stutters.

"Visiting my sister. What's in here?" Victoria shakes the satchel.

The bargirl flushes an even deeper shade, looks down at her feet and mumbles something about supplies, wouldn't want to hear she'd starved, maybe she'll be back sometime.

Victoria makes for the southern end of the city, a wide berth through the ghetto belt with no toes in the church districts, leaves the icon-studded walls of Saragossa late afternoon towards a stretch of ghost towns and older ruins. This funereal path cuts through nameless thatch-roof villages gone decrepit with lack of habitation—fetid remnants of the Plague Year—fields of scrub vegetation and the rusted hulks of beached ships, detritus decreasing until only the rocky desert floor remains punctured by arches of worn white stone.

Somewhere, hounds are baying.

She camps in the prone husk of a decaying MAERSK shipping container, ignoring unpleasant stained holes against its far wall, opens the barmaid's satchel.

A wedge of hard cheese, a crusted loaf of bread, a waterskin, some jerkied fish.

Beneath these, a single-edged knife the length of her hand that she secrets up one sleeve.

Need more flirty servers.

She eats with abandon. Food serves no purpose in the Meridian.

So sated she falls asleep with her head propped on the gunny, wind urging creaks from the rusted hinges of the doors, anxieties pulsing with arterial fervor.

Up early, she comes the following sunrise to a crossroads. Left and right battered tarmac leads into the horizon, dotted sparingly with empty gibbets canted one way or the other. The forward path seems to lead into an edgeless bank of dark fog, as if night has already set only here ahead of her in blasts of smoke—a featureless grey wall tapering into silent black.

She follows through as in the vision La Hija had, never a cough rising despite the smoky air, shadowed shapes looming nearby but never becoming clear.

Abruptly she stands in the dark of full night in an abandoned town sinking into the earth beneath in great buckling ruptures. A sick-looking ochre light reaches from within and Victoria can hear the creak of collapsing metal. Sodium streetlamps bend over the road in predatory arcs. Some of these buildings have fires dying inside of them; others barely resemble the homes or stores they once were, so collapsed are they beneath whatever cataclysm befell this place.

In doorways the decaying corpses of women late in pregnancy leer and lurch, clawed hands clutching, teeth gnashing. Crowns of bone adorn their hairless skulls. Strange patterns trace themselves within their distended torsos.

At the far end of town a stepped stone temple sinks at a sickening angle into the ground. With great difficulty Victoria clambers across the rubble, beset by tittering whispering laughter, until she's standing before the steps and ready to ascend, grateful for the metal handholds that line it. She's panting by the time she crouches next to the sliding metal doors at the pyramid's peak.

A black box is wired to the doors set in the rock, the faint outline of a hand on its screen. Placing her own upon it, red lines scan Victoria's fingerprints and palm lines. With a telegraph chattering it regurgitates a slice of dot-matrix paper she tears off.

```
VICTORIA "COBRA ROJA" NEVARRO
BORN OF PEASANT SOLDIERS UNDER TLALOC'S DAY OF MAZATL
HIGHWAYWOMAN PROFESSIONAL THIEF
BLOOD PHENOTYPE O POSITIVE
PLEASE ENTER WITH THIS RECEIPT IN HAND
```

The doors slide open.

A filthy man, so emaciated it's a wonder he's mobile, sits cross-legged in a flickering ring of melted candles. His head—far too thin a head at that—sits shrouded in bandages stained brown with old blood, a shriveled necklace dangling on his bare chest, clad only in threadbare hakama-like pants of faded red. The man rolls a pair of chipped ivory dice and picks them up again, rolls them and picks them up again. The rusting room is bare of any other decoration.

"I'm looking to pass through," she croaks.

The bandages turn slowly to face her.

"Receipt, please," comes the creaking muffled response. The bandaged man stands and Cobra can only think his arms are just a little bit too long as he reaches over and takes the offered paper.

"Purpose of passage?"

"Visiting family."

The bandages nod over the receipt. "Whoever it is, you won't get them back, but I admire that particular tenacity. You're going to want to swallow one of these straight up, Madam Thief. Not that you're guaranteed passage back, but without this you're lost beyond all measure." He passes over something like a hairless mouse that trembles curled in her palm. She looks from the creature back up to the bandaged man.

"Yes, right now."

With a little trepidation and a couple crunching squeals she consumes it, her mouth raw and coppery. The man sits back down with his dice and gestures to the rear of the room. "Elevator's in the back."

"You're not – *por Dios, eso da asco*– you're not going to…I don't know, judge me or something?"

"Not why I'm here. You've eaten the crynth, your receipt checks out, go on."

She steps around the candle ring and into the clattering wire-cage elevator, punches the one directionless button, and takes a deep breath.

Immediately hit by a wave of nausea, she keeps her constitution in check for the sake of the critical little creature dissolving in her stomach. After several minutes of descent she fights through a massive wave of vertigo that nearly puts her on the floor. It feels instead now like the elevator is ascending, though she can't really be sure. The single lightbulb gutters overhead.

When she steps through the sliding doors and into the salted ashen wasteland, there's no way to tell how much time has passed —a blood-colored sun hangs directly overhead in a sky so hazy grey she'd've thought there was a forest fire near if she didn't know better. She turns briefly to look at the elevator and there's only the suggestion of a weatherworn metal hatch set deep into the sand.

Victoria sights the black toothpick of the Presidio de Calavera nestled on the horizon, jutting out of her deepest nightmares between two all-too-familiar mountain ranges, and she begins her hike.

She passes through scarred igneous wastes like leprous sores on the salt, lightning mumbling and dancing on distant crags in finger-forks of palest blue. She even once sees something with a coyote's ears half as large as one of those far-off peaks blink around a mountain's edge with milky eyes like twin moons before withdrawing again without a sound. She doesn't see it again.

She passes through a dilapidated checkpoint. Inside one squat booth are two very dead men in rotten black and gold livery clutching rifles long gone to rust, bullet holes riddling each leaking corpse and staggered along the crumbling plaster wall behind. In the equivalent building opposite sits a dehydrated cadaver, an ancient thing with a pitted machete in one hand, no visible wounds to speak of. Faded yellow dot-matrix printouts litter the floor. The checkpoint's electric gate is stuck at a forty-five degree angle as if unable to decide whether to lift or stay down, a collapsed bus halfway through the gap painted with the words ROEBUCK COUNTY PRISON SYSTEM.

Victoria knows no such place.

She ducks beneath and moves on.

She passes through a graveyard, an open-air crypt for what could only be giants, slabs of marble and granite in alien configuration humped atop one another in the scrubbed arroyo, the stones larger than houses and crowded around malfunctioning electric lanterns. She thinks it a good place to rest for want of shade but soon enough after stopping comes to hear the distant tinny crying of an infant. A brief investigation reveals no visible life—wary now, she continues along.

She casts her eyes back once and only once to see something lurching amongst the graves.

The black spire growing ever closer, bloated red moon indistinguishable from its daylight sibling.

Now she stands before the Presidio again.

Somewhere up that insidious height sits the cell of Guadalupe Nevarro.

Surreal, seeing the infamous prison without hearing the lap of cold water. The rocks are stained where it once was—beneath the sea line sits an open cave mouth outlined in electric light. It's this she climbs for, hand over hand on the black stone, an unknown time without its ocean mantle and yet still slick to the touch. There are no guards casting spotlights, no murmured orders or shouted commands, just the whistle of wind on ash.

The first inkling of upheaval in her absence comes upon traversal of the subaquatic tunnels.

In a dark hole lit only by a chimney skylight winding into the structure above she confronts an uncountable stack of rotting corpses. The ones at the very bottom naturally are skeletal sludge, the freshest still coagulating on top. Without the resources or stomach to root through the mound she can only hope Lupe isn't somewhere within, but with a shock she does recognize the stringy hair and scarred shoulder of one cadaver cast haphazardly down to the floor.

She rolls it over.

This is Warden de Silva alright – she put that scar there. They couldn't get her into the chair for her transfusion, the daily procedure long a chore for those performing it, and he himself came down to beat her into the manacles. She'd swung with chipped nails and teeth and carved a good one right into his arm. Of all the people to find in a mass grave. All the inhabitants, prisoner and guard alike, might be sliding apart in this reeking pile.

She sees that his face is gone entirely, a featureless blanket of rotting skin.

What happened here?

The natural tunnels lead to the prison morgue, the route up lined with burnt out lamps and gurneys askew and trails of old viscera. There are several objects and machines here in the morgue that suggest more than simple autopsy—pumps of some sort, a mass of wire-choked monitoring equipment. The floor bears two dead Presidio guards but before she can take a good look she's startled by a deep and familiar voice pouring in from elsewhere in the building.

"Angels just above my fingertips."

That voice—ordering guards, cooing over misfortune and wounds inflicted—Warden de Silva's, but it sounds too slow.

"The bridge made this place right."

Victoria enters the ground floor proper, where the cells and the spiral that leads to each block begins, and sees two Presidio guards stripped of uniform and crucified on rotted driftwood. They frame the massive door which leads into the central spire of the prison. Above the jamb are painted the words "BEREISHIT BARA ELOHIM" dried brown—above that perches a klaxon speaker from which de Silva's words drool. The words of a man she's certain is rotting in the basement.

"There's little to no gap in carbon age-dating between the foundation of the Prison and its interior walls."

In the center of the prison a beam of white light spews from the center skylight, exterior conditions be damned, and as Victoria watches stray shards of glass and white dust patter to the floor.

She returns to the spiraling ramp and rubs her arm under its sleeve.

66A-B6N.

A much higher rotation of the passage. The closed cell doors she passes on ascent have a slot where the occupant's name can be affixed and she glances at each hoping that if her sister was moved, she'll see it.

P. Ferdinand.

I. Ortiz.

E. Jawsay.

X. Rosario.

M. Carruthers.

"The Predicants were already here to collect, to hunt, to capture and keep. They taught us with barely a word the sacrifices necessary."

T. Verde.

R. Sanvillerda.

W. Kutsopolous.

H. Quispe.

K. Pena.

"The Predicants showed the gentle transfer that would become a hallmark of my reign, my drive to touch the heavens."

She must be a third of the way up the prison now, almost at a dead run.

66A-B6N.

G. Nevarro.

The door is open.

The cell is empty.

There are fingernail scratches in the walls, in the door, old blood here and there, a dented tin bowl, empty manacles, no Lupe.

"A land of and for the dead is the best place to speak with those up further still."

That son of a bitch. If he's still alive up there, if she's completely mistaken about the corpse in the cellar

taste of blood

then he'll know.

If he doesn't, he'll pay.

See this unlatched office here atop the prison spire, with lush carpets the color of arterial blood, rococo furniture and Surrealist paintings, a phonograph rolling a celluloid cylinder into a microphone.

See the woman slumped in a magnificent chair behind the desk with its lamp-shade of green glass, her head lolling on her shoulders.

Victoria seizes her and lets go almost instantly—this is Lupe but this is not her face, this patchy, misaligned flap of pitted skin.

"No," murmurs Guadalupe, drooling slightly, "no, no, *ya casi termino, estoy bien*, almost back, almost a hundred percent."

"Lupe, please, it's Victoria—I promised I'd be back, *querida*, I'm here now. We're leaving, we're going far away, just like I said. I'm so sorry."

"Victoria," she slurs, spit bubbles forming on her lips.

"That's right, that's right. *Lo siento tanto.* What did they do to you?"

Guadalupe looks up at her, her eyes crossing and uncrossing, and with a sudden wet *schlup* the face slides into focus, aligns itself with the contours of her skull.

It's de Silva.

No wrinkles, more effeminate as it sits upon Guadalupe's face, but it's his features alright, and with a sudden glare Lupe shoots up throwing a punch that sends Victoria prone and bruised, clutching at a broken rib.

"Yes, thank you, all set, *ahora me acuerdo*," says Lupe, removing the needle of the phonograph from its cylinder. "Back to work."

"I did it, Lupe. I got strong for both of us."

"Came back for your darling sister, I see."

"W-What's happened?"

"She's not here!" Lupe screams, insane rage from that terrible mismatched face. "This is mine now!" She grasps at her body, pinching and pulling. "*Mine now.*"

"W-What...?"

"This absolute *clusterfuck*!" yells Lupe, throwing the massive desk chair across the room. "A riot—a *riot*! Twenty guards down before I beat her with a pipe threader."

"You're not Guadalupe."

"You think I spent the last three hundred years like that? I may never live again but I can claw my way up to the core and I *will*."

Suddenly Lupe is right in her face, breath like rotting meat. "Do you remember the thumbscrews, Victoria, the chained cuffs, the Judas Cradle, one thousand cuts filled with shit, brazen bulls and electrodes and manacled chairs? I remember," she whispers.

"Let me show you."

Ice cold water removes Victoria from her catatonia, her arms bound above her in chains, stripped down to her undergarments.

The Warden wears her campaign coat.

"I like it."

Victoria groans absently.

"Big girl words, please. *Aquí todos somos adultos.*"

The Warden walks over to a table laden with rusted tools and crude farming implements, selects the knife that sat up Victoria's own sleeve.

"Cobra Roja, huh? Nobody's ever given me a title cooler than 'the Warden.' Kinda boring."

They slash a line across Victoria's chest and she winces weakly as her undershirt turns red. "I know you're in there somewhere, Guadalupe. De Silva won't finish his work like this. *El no se llevó tu cabeza.*"

"Oh, shut up," scoffs the Warden, slashes the underside of Victoria's left arm, the raw tender flesh of the tricep. "Another day or two to settle in and it'll be back to work, restocking on cattle and handlers. We're so close now." They put the knife down and select a pair of pliers.

"Lupe, please..." and for the first time in years Victoria begins to truly cry in earnest.

"Knock that off."

"Lupe, I love you!" she sobs. "*Te quiero, hermana!*"

With a lightning-quick motion the Warden reaches up with the pliers and yanks one of Victoria's healthy incisors from her mouth, claret gushing as she flails on her chain. A sudden shock of clarity comes over the Warden's features and they slowly turn to stare at the pliers in their hand, back up at Victoria.

"Come back, Lupe, please."

The Warden drops the pliers.

"*Tu puedes hacerlo.*"

They reach up with one hand and punch themselves in the face hard enough to fall to the chamber floor. Victoria swings gently, breath baited, blood rushing to stain her clothes. A string of drool descends from her lower lip.

"She almost had me, *eso está claro!*" says the Warden, climbing unsteadily to their feet. "I could hear her in the back of my head!

Back on track."

The Warden grins as they replace the pliers with a set of wood-handled shears.

Sometime later the Warden washes their hands with cool water and a linen rag.

No need for security again just yet. Soon the black water will complete its five-year low tide and return rushing to cover the dead land beneath once more, and work will begin again in earnest.

The Warden's making their way up through the morgue when their feet stop moving entirely. First thought is to check the floor but the stone here's the same as anywhere else, cold, static, normal.

Somewhere, someone is screaming.

Who the fuck else is here?

The Warden's swinging arms freeze in place as if held by the wrists. Their lips then, clasped by invisible fingers.

Guadalupe.

Somewhere, the shrieking.

Guadalupe!

In the back of the Warden's head, Guadalupe is screaming at the top of her lungs, such a mindless howl of sorrow and pain that headaches begin generating in clusters around the inside of the Warden's head, clamoring needles of red-hot hate.

GODDAMN IT WOMAN, NO TE ATREVAS!

And then even conscious thought begins to peter out as the Warden's mind is gripped by the vise-like wail of agony within.

As the first trickles of black water begin whispering across the ash, the dim red sun sneaking up the horizon to replace the vigil of its nocturnal sister—

The Warden remains still as the foundation's stone, now and forever, as hangs the corpse of Cobra Roja beneath the Presidio de Calavera.

IN THE
HINTERLANDS

I think the shady advertise their presence via scent.

Olfactory anxiety, like when your ride starts making that stink and you just know the fucker's about to spend a week in the shop.

Radiates off quacks like midday heat.

The man in the rickety swivel chair before my desk, Mesannepada, sends off thick spirals. Cigarette smoke swirls in Mandelbrot loops every time he gestures, hands like ruddy steaks, brown suit like the carpeting in a district attorney's office. Salt-and-pepper scruff dusts his sagging jowls, circular high-prescription glasses direct attention towards dark, somehow insectoid little eyes. His gut is making substantial claims on a cracked leather belt despite the more-than-generous efforts by a supplementary pair of clip-on suspenders to keep just such an event from occurring. Mesannepada is, to put it lightly, a pig in business clothes.

"See it's actually really easy. You and your toadies take your grubby fingers and carve the zone in the charter upload. You plant the telectropneumic scanning plug—the one you mysteriously lost—right in the middle and feed us every chirp of data, atmospheric *and* seismic. Then competent employees come recover."

I cough. "I *do* know how to do my job."

"Do you? Oh, that's excellent news. Really great."

The statuesque stunner behind the desk is yours truly District Supervisor Fletcher Prince, Outpost ED3 Martense: Hinterlands, Throckwyndle & Brine Expansion Incorporated.

Okay fine, the Kinski-eyed five-five brunette with the missing pinkies.

Fuck you, I'm anxious.

Mesannepada isn't the sort of man I talk to directly unless there's a serious problem. When in the situation our outpost is, your parent corporation sends whoever it must to make abundantly clear nothing pertinent is light-hearted—our situation so un-light-hearted at this juncture that if it weren't an abstract thing it'd crush our jumpjet. We're in some shit and I know it. Our statistic output defines pitiful better than an orphanage sweatshop.

Mesannepada nods. "Just wasn't sure since we haven't had quota upload of any sort whatsoever in...what was it, D?"

"Two months." Dumuzid, Mesannepada's curator.

This guy's another story entirely. One ear hangs on his boss's spiel but it's clear the rest of his body has its own agenda. Sunken eyes dart from window to boss to floor to me to the window again, mouth a liver-colored slash across a face like a china plate, pale and washed-out with regal shaven cheekbones. The seersucker suit and black cravat he wears are impeccably sterile, as is the gigantic Miller positron gunbutt jutting from beneath his left arm. A man who surely goes home to an unadorned apartment and sits drinking water before sleeping with his limbs folded like the deceased. If Mesannepada is a pig, then Dumuzid is a falcon, a predatory bird whose obvious talents are surpassed only by his zeal to use them.

"Two fucking months." Mesannepada drops the act. "What are you guys doing out here, really? If we put your output on a big scatter plot, scatterchart, whatever, the slope or rather the trend excuse me just goes down. Embassy employees are starting to get turned away at the door, huge no-no there. You were doing alright. What the hell happened?"

I lean back in my chair and look up through the plastiglass skylight where their corporate cruiser idles with a throaty hum, a mean gunmetal thing fat with beetle-shark imagery tethered to our building with a half-mile length of rusting anchor cable. I'm inked hard because this was supposed to be an easy-ass nowhere job and lately it's been anything but. You won't find any paraphernalia here, though. "Got a little rough lately. Town ain't what it used to be, loonies out in the jungle, you know? I been barking up your tree some months about arming us."

Mesannepada shakes his head and the chair creaks ominously. "And we've been throwing back every memo that says you *can't* have weapons, company policy, there's already lightning on your survey craft. You ignoring those at your convenience?" Bullshit, if you believe Severin's eye-witness insistence that equivalent teams mapping the warrens beneath Mercury get a Miller pistol per unit.

I shake my own. "And I'm telling *you* guys, when we get down on foot to plant your magic plug, we nearly get ambushed by whatever leftover fuckups still run around outside rubbing sticks together."

"I don't want to know what kind of reprobate bullshit you're up to out here, Prince—mother of god you better get that plug back, plant the sonofabitch, and give us a good solid grid reading or I will kick your shit back in the dirt."

"You the cops?"

"I don't like your attitude."

"I'm not fucking selling it."

Dumuzid nods slowly. Mesannepada's knuckles turn white but the other man's already leaned down, whispering furiously in his ear.

"You do know dangerous equipment recovery isn't part of my job description, right?" Mesannepada puts a palm towards my face.

Rude.

The fatter man sighs when the thinner finishes whispering, the chair squealing beneath him.

"Given your abject failure, you get to say fuck-all in my book. D tells me you're not completely unfamiliar with violence so if things come down to that, we're glad Too Tall Freeman's leading the charge. I'm informed we've also a lunch with my immediate superiors on this very topic. Glad we talked, Fletch; would've hated to bring the Court bad news."

"I try not to disappoint."

"I am—*Judas Priest, fix this fucking chair*—I am under the impression you can operate like a motivated adult, so rather than force my curator here to shadow this little expedition, I'll only have him check in on your assigned jump frequency."

"How sweet."

"Be as smart an ass as you want, Prince, because when there's *still* no fresh data sliding across my tablet, I'm going to laugh choking off the whole fucking loose end."

They unass my office. I call dealing with that a day's work.

Time for ink.

When I do get up and outdoors, a few grumbling clouds drift across the dusky Venusian sky as their cruiser makes the final phase of its start-up cycle. The anchor cable has long since retracted and the ship drifts idly in no particular direction. I'm kind of surprised a T&B company khan that level would show face in as shifty a barony sector as Martense, as backwater a district as the Hinterlands.

I sit down on the pocked roof next to our dish web with a pack of Ink-laced cigarettes, pondering as the engine cones flare white. To be honest I rarely come up here—I'm no repair tech—but it's quiet and that's good right now, that's good stuff. Inked hard, I can see everything outlined in razor contrast—the shimmering red neon, the heavy-eyed customers with wandering stares, the snarling wire-wrapped truck grills less than a mile to the northeast—Martense, Venus's most forgettable prospecting town-turned-rookery. T&B owned the real estate for a good decade, ran a bunch of cheapo terraforming surveys with offworld labor until the Chinese government bought out the whole continent. These days the corporation's only Venusian holdings are this outpost and a commercial embassy in town. After the Chinese courts had less luck than our company with the former residents they pretty much deserted the territory of manpower, so now it's a leftover pit of unruly expat rejects from myriad miscellaneous backgrounds and occupations come to circle the drain.

With a godless roaring bang Mesannepada's ship tears a hole in the atmosphere and jumps through it, sending a blast of humid wind across the jungle. Ramona, our modified jump pilot, opens the roof hatch and nails me with inverted cybernetic eyes—black sclera, white iris—as our hair is blown askew. "Chalk Ninety-Nine back online per request. Nasty storm projected from the quarantine wall tonight."

I exhale black smoke. "I'll be down. Tomorrow we're on Fortuna X."

"I remember, if I may be so bold, your words something like, '*We comb one more vacant deadly map square in the next year and I'm kicking it.*' Then we hit Ursus Red and you smiled and wiped your hands."

"T&B gentry came through with his pet monkey today. Told me either we recover that stupid scanner and read the grid or we're all out of here. They're checking up on us soon as we launch. I don't know about you but I kind of inked all my money away, so this is uh, this is where I'm at. I can handle myself without steady work, but I owe it to you guys to keep it going, right? I'm the one who said we'd be ignored."

Ramona shrugs. "Dunno. Tough break, your call, really. You know those ex-terraformers are heavy metal out Fortuna X-ways?"

"Yeah, I know." I shudder from ink and memory. Ramona's face undulates softly. "Severin still has that crate under his bed, I hope."

"I'll ask. Probably should keep that from the company."

"I'll be down after I finish this. See if we have anything left to eat."

The sky burns ochre next morning as we routine through the dawn. Bare feet wading through discarded inkjars and empty boxes of rolling papers, tins of shag hollowed of content, unwashed laundry, overturned oyster pails. The understaffed Outpost has been hemming and hawing about obtaining what we consider an unobtainable performance level set by our disgruntled corporate masters. Under my advisory, we've—at least, I have—been enjoying our unnoticed backwater here for a while. Couldn't tell you what made the company take a sudden interest in our decline, but we'll run this shit quick and throw them off for a while again if we can.

If we can't, I'll own it.

At breakfast, I turn to Rudolph Severin as he slurps the last of his noodle supplement. "We're gonna need that crate under your bunk, if you still have it."

He nods a jiggling mouthful. "Ramona asked last night. I moved it into the jumper earlier."

"Cool."

Ramona herself appears and jettisons a globe of black coffee. "You ink yet?"

"Not happening today," Severin responds, standing to sink his dishes.

"Don't get sick. Don't need that."

"Can't feel any sicker, to be honest."

"Take a little if you feel like you need it."

I am not of this mindset—I *will* be inking before we take off.

Grubjet Chalk Ninety-Nine and its hangar are most of the Outpost—the bunks and office, kitchenette bathroom, and monitoring station are all arranged atop the building, maybe to prioritize architectural parsimony or something. As a result the launch tongue for the jet *is* the hangar floor, which extends electrically to the exterior. The jumper is a squat bat-thing, VTOL engines tucked neatly against the chassis, skeletal wing arms and tail slicked back for aerodynamic purposes beyond my knowledge. It used to be white—years of use before and including us have blasted it a filthy rusted no-color, the only markings still distinguishable the huge once-red-now-flaky-brown "C-99"s painted on the top of the wing and the sides of the fuselage.

All necessary combing equipment is within—the jet is a tool as much as the scanners are. Lockers crammed in a corner of the hangar hold environment equipment but other than that our telemetric beacons and seismographs are all compartmentalized within the jumper. Ramona splits an inkstick with me before we go, Severin holding up his personal promise to attempt the assignment sober and beginning the charge-up process. The engines hum to orange as we fill the room with black smoke.

Ramona settles into her pilot rig, a goggled helmet wired to the roof of the cockpit. Flicking a number of switches, the jet whines in response to her psychoelectric signal as systems power to ready. Pulling the lenses over her face she flashes us a thumbs up.

Soon as the pad extends the Grubjet leaps away, tongue retracting beneath. Ramona levels out and shoots us low over the semi-terraformed jungle. Punching up Fortuna quadrant X on the dash she activates the coolant feedback loop. Severin is adjusting his beacons, a black wooden crate with yellow stripes tucked under his seat. The treetops that reach from below have begun to salsa and I know the ink is hitting.

"Got a company call."

I bet we fucking do. "Punch it through."

An image of Dumuzid fades into view on the opposite wall of

the cabin. "Supervisor Prince. On your way bright and early, good to see," he drawls.

"Yes sir that's us, bright and good, on our way, so early. Fortuna X doesn't stand a chance and neither do we."

"Your complaints were registered with the embassy. You can speak with HR as always regarding assignment of further personnel. As to the degenerate inhabitants of the semi-sectors, I don't doubt the sound of bleating sonar will send them scampering into their caves."

Ramona and I laugh. "You read those complaints? Ursus Red and Queen Catherine Ridge? We've been begging for months, apparently against policy, for something to defend ourselves with."

Dumuzid is silent for a few moments, smirking. "Radio when you reach the area of operation, Supervisor. Curator out."

Severin slowly shakes his head. "Corporate."

"Probably still listening." I don't want this opportunity going belly-up for something petty like overheard snark.

Severin points to the dash. "What're they saying?"

"*Compay pongase duro*," calls Ramona, who can't lean or turn to look at us from her nest of blinking lights and cables.

"I don't know how you can stand this."

"It's cool old culture, you gotta *feel* it, man."

"That the ink or you talking?"

"One and the same, brother."

I narrow my eyes at Severin.

"Sounds like your feet are getting a little cold."

Severin shrugs but doesn't say anything.

Ramona brakes the jumpjet rapidly at that moment. A plump strip of jet from nose to belly has been smothered in sensor equipment and one very special T&B toy we're all big fans of—a military-grade chemical arc battery intended for defoliation and minor surface drilling. We've also found it useful for dissuading assailants, keep ours pumped with a smuggled industrial propellant, gives it a lot more bang for the buck. I've seen creepers tear off into the trees half-torched from a brush and I've seen a psychotic amok grilled stem to stern by full energy discharge.

There's a comforting hum as the arc battery and surveillance gear power on. Then Ramona is taking us down slowly, the Grubjet swaying ever so slightly from side to side as she inks out on her music.

I stand, turn to Severin. "Let's go with the regular. I know it's a slog but there's no sense in fucking off."

"Interesting choice of words. Trenchant insight."

"You wanna fucking talk about it? Or you wanna mouth off like a little bitch, Rudy? What's it gonna be?"

"We wouldn't *be* here if we hadn't spent two months tripping at your bequest. The damage isn't worth it. I can't believe I let you guys talk me into taking years off my life."

"You decided yourself to go with, and obviously enjoyed it," from the cockpit.

"Truer words, but there's something to be said for fucking pressure when you live with your boss." Then he turns, the jet having reached a six foot hover, and jumps into the whispering yellow shrubs. I follow him down with his thoughts bouncing against my own. This outburst seems to have come out of nowhere, but Severin's mood swings have been a problem since before we inked. He's probably been dwelling on this for two weeks in a haze.

"Do your beacon thing. I'm going to scan the radius real quick."

"Don't get lost."

I let that roll off me.

Gonna do this the old-fashioned way, with my drugged-up peepers. I lift my environment visor, really just a flexible forehead brace that attaches to the suit for holographic information displays, and pull on my domino mask. Then I drag the visor down.

Fletcher Prince on the job.

There are dried clawmarks in the ground here, old ones. Dad had a farm and I'd follow the clattering tractor sometimes, stepping in tracks just like these in the cloying hay. In the right season the Venusian grasses dry a bit and that similar smell takes me right back; I'll lose myself standing on the roof for fifteen minutes stoned just sniffing deep and remembering the barn and hot wood smoke and the comforting heat of animal proximity. Once I was so gone I got hit by a drop of chemical rain and nearly lost an eye trying to scramble in beneath the Lansky field. Got a funky scar by my left temple for that one, a fine addition to my collection.

Some of Venus' finest flora are on the docket today, a cluster of vampiric weeds off to my left filling the air with crimson mist, a creeper vine making serpentine progress in the wet soil below. The usual suspects. The weeds are obvious to detect and thus easy to avoid; only someone with both thumbs in their ass could stumble through the vampiric psychoactives. As for the creeper, well, three people can probably yank the fucker to pieces if it acts a fool, never mind if the battery hits it.

The immediate area is clear for probing.

The first subsection of Quadrant X is sort of a cleared land cove, a cul-de-sac of low scrub brush jutting off the shallows of the toxic Queen Catherine River. An ancient basalt pillar pitted with weather and time marks the start of the Hinterlands, a wet forest with a density that puts mangroves to shame. Venusian trees grow thick and gnarled with bark and foliage a deep green-black. We hate it in here because the secondary terraformers cut their disenfranchised employees loose when bankruptcy hit. The panic-mad planetscapers have been living in the ultradense jungle like murderous Merry Men, grovelling to the plant life and making the place hell for any successive holdings. These are the very same devolved jackoffs who somehow managed to get their hands on our primary piece of scanning tech.

No cultish psychos here, but markings around the base of the pillar coincide with similar ones we've seen on survey indicating a territory is near, just as Ramona said. The day is quiet, the sky sweltering with that all-encompassing yellow Venusian tint. Severin is grinding the last of his telemetry spikes into the ground in a fat-angled semicircle. When he links them together the beacons will give us a decent motion ping.

I channel in Ramona. "What's it look like up there?"

"No foliage disturbance on targ, starting to get decent readings from Severin. We're on the clock and moving at our usual. Same shit." I can hear music bouncing beneath her response.

"Good to hear. Tell Dumuzid and we'll move on."

I flash Severin a thumbs up. He nods at me, then makes a motion over his face with one palm and shakes his head. He's making fun of my mask. Least it seems he's feeling better.

Little manual labor'll do that.

We meet below the thrumming jet.

"Give us a stripe right up the riverbank, Rami, we'll put a marker where it turns into swamp. Quarantine Wall starts about a half mile after anyway."

Ramona cranks the arc battery up with a warbling hum. There's a mechanical pop and then an ear-shattering detonation as a bolt of blood-colored lightning fries a wide row of tangled scrub and tree, the growth bursting into terrible white flame and crumpling to ash in seconds. We move up this charred column to plant a projection antenna on the north end of the chaparral, match it to the telemetric frequency of the spike beacons and give Ramona a cursory but sufficient box on her radar to work with.

So the fun begins.

We've drilled the projector into the almost-soggy ground with its corkscrew base, Rudy and I, when Ramona's voice cuts through the earpiece. "Somebody watching from the treeline."

Chills run down my neck in the noon humidity as we both see a pair of legs disappearing into the darkness of the jungle. With ink irradiating my bloodstream I can't tell whether or not I saw the trees sort of gather the figure back in. "Of course," says Severin, alternately wringing his hands and attempting to prime the antenna. "No, of course, I mean why not? Why fucking not, though, really?"

"Shut up," I offer, thumb through to Ramona. "What do you think?"

"Gimme a sec to reel back." *Whir whir.* "Definitely a person."

Fuck me. "Fuck me."

"My thoughts exactly. Can I be honest?"

"I prefer it."

"Either the cameras are wonk or something else is going on, because—"

"What do you mean *something else?*" cuts Severin.

"—because that guy's body moved real weird."

I activate the antenna system with a programmed code from my wrist monitor. "What's your read on that?"

"Ah it's uh...it's pretty clear. There's definitely movement further in. Limited seismic from Rudy's spikes're telling me we should be able to follow a series of those pillars down a jagged line to the southeast, keeps movement to our left."

"Where does that bring us?" asks Severin, and I see the lid over his steel-colored right eye is twitching spasmodically.

"Out in a fair shot from Martense with like, forty-five percent of the Hinterlands skim-scanned."

I shake my head. Severin opens his mouth and I pull his brakes right then and there. "Absolutely not. We need at least seventy-five to look like we fucking tried, *and* we need that stupid plug."

Both of my team members are silent. Behind us in the midst of this exchange the river murmurs vitriolic khaki mud in belches that cover the rustling of brush. I don't know how long he's been there, but out of the corner of my eye I can suddenly see someone crouching again at the treeline.

"Rami – the coords-"

The scrub by the figure flares red-white under a brilliant needle of explosive electricity.

"Running biologicals...he's dead or he peaced. Nothing now."

Jesus.

"Rudy, your crate is our last resort, but we're going to end up using the fucker, I'm almost certain. We'll survey as best we can and as much as we can. When it gets a little hot, a little heavy, we break the crate. Hotter and heavier than that and we're out, alright? Gotta give it a shot."

"Suddenly you're all business again."

I shake my head at him. "You *don't* want me trying to salvage this?"

He glowers.

"Now's really not the fucking time for lip. Ramona, guide us down the pillars. We'll keep reading as we go. Keep the battery primed."

Severin grumbles forward, brick-like palm computer held before him and linked to our surveillance equipment. Just a big chunk of digital memory made to record and store beacon feed. As we begin our trek through the tenebrous thicket, signal-boosted telemetry records the ground underfoot and its floral makeup, the general topographical and geographical feel of the area, limited seismic readings. We're supposed to buff the quality and range of the reading to a phenomenal extent with the plug scanner. These we'll upload, triplicate, and beam out to Dumuzid, Mesannepada, and T&B Expansion Archives with the appropriate submission tags.

Then they can all suck my cock.

We've made a headway of about thirty percent in, three pillars coddled in ash behind us, when a warped figure tilts to standing from prone in the scrub clearing we're working through. It begins to lurch forward, marionette vibes with its broken-joint stagger. I radio Ramona and gesture from the ground, "Let's see what we're dealing with real quick. Don't shoot yet."

I want to know what to expect here.

It's only a few steps before I see something's very wrong.

Above the eyes the top of the man's skull, for it is or was a man, has broken into an enormous blossom of veiny cobalt petals, the pistil bed its own rotted brain. Bare-skinned except for threadbare workboots and a pair of filthy striped boxer-briefs, its chest bears a frayed leather buckle beneath a crude dried sun of braided grasses, bracketed dashes carved scar-dark into the flesh around it.

Despite all this, a voice scrapes from within, lips pulling back from teeth long gone black.

"*Zweck?*"

I look back at Severin.

"*IHR ZWECK HIER?*"

"Uh just passing through, on our way now, off we go," and I begin to strafe around the flower man in a wide radius. Blood is pounding in my throat, ink and anxiety a poorly churning blend. Severin is frozen in place but Ramona is beginning to hover toward me. She whispers over the mic, "Fry it do I fry it want me to fry it boss fry it or what man 'cause-"

"One sec."

Glowering at Rudy it screams, "*EINDRINGLING!*"

It seizes and Severin is screaming on the ground flailing through the grass as Ramona blasts stone from the pillar, chemical lightning punching off chunks of ancient rock as the man crawls on all fours up and around it head petals closing, foliage falling off in ashen clumps. Reaching the top it leaps towards the Grubjet. Ramona sears the air crimson as it stretches something near six feet to shatter the windshield.

Landing on all fours in a rolling crouch, the flower man scampers into the trees with preternatural speed as the jumpjet pitches.

I think that might have been his tongue.

There's a thorn the size of my thumb sticking out of Severin's bare left cheek right beneath the eye when I get to him. Tiny crimson roots are starting to spread from the tip towards the socket as I yank it out. Rudy shrieks as the feelers disappear beneath the flesh of his face.

Over the radio, Ramona's yelled, "What the fuck is that," twice and I see Chalk Ninety-Nine's right wingspan slam into a wall of treetop, the cockpit disappearing under some throbbing multicolored mass. As Severin's now conscious and breathing, I run towards the jet as it belly-flops onto the ground with a cringe-inducing series of metal bangs and crunches, smoke coming from the port turbine.

"Ramona! Rami!" I tear at the cockpit door. The blood-and-bark colored mass of pulsing cerebral roots atop the face of the jet gurgles at me and I tear at that, too, slick clumps of something that feels like cold wet mud falling apart in my hand. I get the door off the hinge and unhook Ramona, drag her out through the frame.

A trickle of blood runs from her nose but those creepy baby whites are moving, if dazed. "Just a little clock-cleaning. I'm cool. Got the helmet off before the feedback."

I help her stand all the same. She braces herself on her knees and takes a few deep breaths.

"Rudy okay?"

I point to where he's sitting up in the grass, picking at the weeping hole in his face.

"What do we do now?"

"You seen that shit before?"

Rami scowls. "He had the thing on his chest but the flower – never seen that. Dodged lightning and hit me with his fucking *tongue*. I can't...that's fucked."

"I'll make our report. Take your supplements, hydrates, anything survival-oriented. Strip the jet while I figure out Rudy."

Ramona is whaling on the cockpit with a shovel as I help Severin to standing and walk him back to the fallen jumper. He moans when he sees it. "We're done."

"I'll help you. Whatever you need, alright?"

"Save the last bullet for yourself."

"Shut the fuck up, we're not gonna die. We'll keep moving in as much open space as possible, get that emergency alert going, stay visible. Grab your crate. Ain't no thang but a chicken wang."

"Don't wanna see a chicken's wang," he mumbles, dragging the crate out of the jumper wreck.

The biomass has dissolved most of the prow with a throaty gurgle so we move to the base of the pillar and crack open Severin's toy. I pull out the matte metal braces and 'trodes, the band and straps, the ceramic shield, the handgrip, the tank. Though he keeps scratching at the dry hole under his eye, complaining of tightness in his chest, Rudy helps us construct the thing and wire it to my head, reading off a fat yellowed manual of Cyrillic characters. He explains as we go that he purchased the Shatterback under the table from a wizened labor heavy who'd miraculously earned his ticket back to Earth. The old worker grumbled in accented English that the solid spear of molten virus the head-mounted Shatterback fired was designed for carving howling diseases away from the tender organ bounty of the Venusian throatmines—natural tissue farms—no harm done to the crop with the right punchcards slotted in. As the bolt is projected through a transneural psionic resonator, the throatmines of Banyuk Plateau found its frequencies equally useful for breaking away ambered biotic slag in great swathes. The man then somberly went on to describe another use he'd seen amidst a penitentiary riot.

Rudy refuses to share this element.

We get it assembled and strap the Shatterback around my head with little argument from an obviously envious Severin, who knows its usefulness would be diminished in his current condition. He does help insert four slotted yellow punchcards of virus crystal into the armpiece. I pop an inkstick which Ramona eventually drags from despite her anxiety, Rudolph reluctantly puffing to dull his pain.

Then we move.

We make only around a mile's progress to the south by Ramona's wrist navigator, the little emergency alert bleating with all its tiny might. Clearings have rapidly become a pipedream, the jungle beginning to close around us in force. I'm just starting to sift into my high despite circumstance before Severin drops to his knees clutching his chest.

"Shit, I shouldn't have smoked, I don't feel...oh." He turns with terrible dull vacancy on his face.

"That mask is so stupid, Fletch."

Then he caves in, deflating completely like an emptied balloon, as if he never had organs or bones to speak of. The wrinkled skin on the ground with red-black dust wisping from the empty eyes looks more like a Rudy Severin costume than anything else. Ramona starts screaming.

"Hey okay I know shush shut the fuck up it'll hear us! I know!" I press her against a gnarled black tree. "Shut. It. Down. I know. Don't think about it, just keep moving, and let's keep it fucking *quiet*."

She nods, hyperventilating, then stops and stares. Her eyes grow enormous. I'm about to ask her what when suddenly I can hear it too, a bass chanting, a sort of rustling, sort of croaking. The same thing repeated over and over, coming from the trees around us. First the top of this one, then behind that one, then far, then near, never placeable.

"*Aus meinem haus. Aus meinem kopf. Aus meinem haus...aus meinem kopf.*"

I'm unfamiliar with the language and tone but I'm not too high to know it's whatever the flower thing spoke in. Guttural and deep, fitting speech for plants. Ramona puts her fingers to her temples, her eyes rolling. "What the fuck is that."

"I don't know."

"*Aus meinem haus, aus meinem kopf.*"

"What is it saying."

"*—aus meinem kopf.*"

"I don't fucking speak plant or whatever, Rami, I don't know."

"Oh god, it's everywhere—the Ridge wasn't like this..."

"*Aus meinem haus—*"

"Ramona..."

"*Aus meinem kopf.*"

"It's *in* the *fucking trees*!"

Bolting into the woods, the chant grows in volume as she disappears from sight. I follow her as best I can until I'm tracking only muffled sounds of struggle. These begin to dim as well.

Silence.

I wrap my fingers around the power-stud grip of the Shatterback and squeeze. With a whining hum it shudders to life around my head, faceplates powering on, bathing the jungle a jaundiced glow. I concentrate hard on my intent to clear the area and proceed to defoliate the flora in a tunnel before me with a single sickblast, vegetation shriveling to black dust under the crackling yellow spear with a death-rattle sigh, my head knocked back from the force of firing. Running best I can with unfamiliar roots and mud underfoot I pass dense trunks darker than oil and twisted beyond compare, arthritic clutches of tortured branch and limb draped in wet green-black mosses, following what's broken or stomped, hoping it's Ramona doing the breaking and stomping. The yawning gaps in the bark could be weathered hollows, could be screaming faces. I'm too stoned and high-wound to know, my eyes thudding in their sockets with adrenaline.

I'd say I was scared shitless, and I guess I am to be honest, but you have to understand—you see some serious shit growing up on a farm. Never mind when you spend half a decade homeless after twice that in the service, "honorable discharge" but not a hand of help in sight, near feral in the catacombs below Kowloon-2. Missing fingers as proof. I've had ample time to come to terms with fear and the fact that as gripping and paralyzing as it is, as difficult to handle as it can be, you ignore the panic and try to use the fear itself, the alertness it brings, or there's no chance for you, none whatsoever.

Ahead is a chipped ceramic sign slung between two trees with copper wire—spacecraft salvage?

Scrawled in something long dried black is the word KUMENITES.

Beyond this a shape moves amongst the trunks.

The flower man is on all fours in the scrub, shuddering as if out of breath. At my approach it turns to look at me with head petals open, crimson roots having broken through most of the facial orifices sometime since I saw it last. The head extends five feet on a neck stretched sinewy and snakelike by roots wrapped into the flesh, repurposed vertebrae breaking out of the shriveled stem of its throat like white thorns. It makes no sound, just assesses me with root-filled sockets before scampering away on all fours up a tree, neck S-coiled in on itself. I blow a rotting chunk out with the Shatterback but it's already rustling unseen amongst the treetops.

The head rockets out from the leaves overhead with tensed muscle and snaps its jaws before retracting. I'm so amped up I've already chewed through one whole punchcard with just two blasts. I send two thinner spears of light into the canopy where it was—my reward is a hollow rasping as a single arm gone black and yellow at the joint falls from above.

Then we're off, branches and debris a breadcrumb trail to follow at a sprint, the flower man racing one-armed through the jungle with little difficulty. The trail gets thicker as distance adds signs of habitation to the mix. I begin seeing dozens upon dozens of empty spheroid jars with labels of Chinese calligraphy, scorch marks blackening the forest floor littered with shattered ceramic like broken teeth, loops of colored wiring reclaimed by the soil.

I burst into a strange glade—a clearing with no light from overhead, dense branches intertwined above leaving the forest floor bare. An ancient starship hulk covered in more fading calligraphy leans nose up in the clearing center against a structure far older, hollow fuselage an arched edifice into a mausoleum-esque box hewn of shimmering stone like pale obsidian.

In the darkness something flails.

Twitching beneath Ramona's body.

She's been stripped and hung carelessly from her feet, blood running down the long-stained stone into a faded drain of green copper, spattering over the flower man. Roots wind from the gored stump of its arm, bulging as the body drinks deep. At my approach the neck twists up and around and I see Ramona's eyes jammed crudely into its own deformed sockets, held in place and manipulated by clusters of red roots. My stomach heaves and the shuddering thing crunches to its feet, petals around the brain opening as the rotting organ inside begins to mutter with diseased orange light.

In my panicked state I lay down a blinding two-card assault that hurls me against the trunk of a nearby tree. The flower man decomposes in a single shrieking yellow instant, flesh shriveling and blasting off the bone as that too crumbles to ashen dust. At the same second a hoarse wailing fades from the jungle, a sudden gust as the blighted soot dissipates into thin air.

With some difficulty I lay Ramona against a tree and do the same to her, eyes closed, holding the beam long enough to be sure she's gone before I open them.

The base of the tree is smeared with black and grey, nothing more.

The stone cube bears the last horror.

Immediately past the draining room I take a scuffed flight of stairs down, walls illuminated by my visor light. At the bottom lies a small chamber tilting at an angle into the ground. The furthest corner is piled with human shit. On a stack of Venusian straw opposite— that fucking smell—lie a series of datascreens, a chronology of the development of datascreens from ancient to recent.

The earliest say things like UNTERNEHMENS NACHRICHTEN. After that are a number with Chinese characters on them. All are maps of different jungle quadrants marked with coordinate points, these connected by line into abstract shapes. The most recent say T&BE, INC. These two are marked by axis point with locations I recognize as near our outpost.

What the fuck is this?

Under a draped piece of stitched cloth that looks a bit too much like leather is a humming blue ball with three mechanical legs and an antenna.

The goddamn plug.

Something smashes into the back of my head and sends me to the floor, breaks my headlamp. Feels like they near knocked my eyes out of my sockets. The face-pieces of the Shatterback go clattering onto the floor and the whole rig sends a shock through my temples as whoever hit me stomps on the plates. When I'm able to open my eyes again I'm banging against the carven stairs as a woman with wild hair drags me back out into the fading daylight of the jungle.

"Ramona?"

She lets go and turns.

No, I don't recognize this long-dead cadaver with the half-melted skin. A raspy howl and it darts out a tongue like an opposable tentacle, cracked dry and weeping, chokes me against the ground by my throat. I try to tear it off, both hands slipping on clammy ridges. The face peels open in veiny cobalt petals as the rotting root-infused tissue beneath exhales a cloud of bright crimson mist into my face.

Colors that shouldn't mix begin to anyway, treetops melting up in thick runners until the sky is a sick green-black. Yellow fog gasps from the ground as my head groans with hangover pounding. The corpse that restrains me holds both hands out before it palm up and though I see nothing in them, a blue holographic screen identical to those projected by our late jumpjet flickers into view.

Dumuzid is lighting a cigarette. I was wondering why he hadn't called. His voice is deeper than before; maybe it's the mist, maybe the ink. "I like science facts and stuff. How 'bout you?"

My mouth opens and closes as if on a hinge.

Black roots slither up from the wet mud and clamp my arms tight against my sides, digging deep into the skin.

"Kumenites are a mutation of Venus' vampiric weeds – around when we ditched the early terraformers, the whole genus decided to advance longevity by using people to feed instead of feeding on people. They've been adding up, slowly I understand, picking off kidnapped stragglers and other freaks that haven't gotten the root yet."

The flower woman's tongue reels up slowly to wet the insides of its face-petals.

"They actually survey the place themselves via pillar by the tenets of nature worship, if you can believe it. Something to do with guiding the growth of a deity tree. The Chinese used to offer up a systems engineer and a metric fuckload of smoked plum to get mapping on the cheap."

"You gave them the plug."

"We don't have *that* many resources to spare per se but we do have a survey team putting up bad numbers, a reputation to keep, disgruntled embassy employees we can coerce into misplacing equipment."

"Why—are you—telling me all this?"

"Christ, come on Prince, you're not stupid, you just make bad decisions. Give yourself a second to put it together if you have to."

The hologram blips out of existence.

The horror above closes its petals beneath the warping sky and lurches onto all fours, face above my own and for a moment it *does* look like Ramona before it turns to Severin's then melts back into a decaying nightmare.

With a stuttered howl the root restraints drag me beneath the reeking sludge.

LOVE & DEATH VS. THE MOLE PEOPLE

Night brings blood, brown in yellow light.

From the watchtower he can see them scrambling from their warrens, some on all fours others striding upright, eyes glittering in the dim electric glow. He cuts the cassette player short and crouches on the platform's uneven wooden floor with his rifle. Chambering a cartridge he eyes the foremost figure and squeezes off a round that clips its torso, sending it spinning to the ground in a little burst of flame.

He can hear other guns opening up around the pits.

Someone gets a flare up, casting lichens in sulfurous radiance. The figures burn and fall, chop and shriek and feed. He throws the bolt and fires, throws the bolt and fires, tries to aim as best he can in the dark with shaking hands. The screaming is as real as always. The no man's land around the sinkholes is a perpetually charred and bloody tundra of muddied earth and bodies.

Artillery gets going from somewhere beneath, great globs of *something* coughed from below that burn dark stinking craters in the cave floor. The figures are starting to retreat, some dragging dead or wounded behind as their big guns take the weight off. He can head back down the ladder, back down to different varieties of warmth.

His plan is to make tea and try to block out the yelling and that plan is canceled by a tumorous slug from an enemy sling, a great reeking fist that brings the watchtower down in a hail of planks and splinters and buries his body beneath.

The player is all she sticks around for.

Swann and Treeworth stay to dig through the timbers for ammunition and maybe the good Sergeant's body, Chorba rummaging about for the dead man's cigarettes or chocolate, but all Chincoteague needs to see is the cassette player. It's blackened on one side but miraculously still operable. They'll need music, one of the only escapes in the Aghartan Drift.

The Subterran Union have been waging an expansion campaign into the depths beneath their cavern home now for two years. The targets of their landlust are the mineral deposits and aquifers that seismic excavation has promised below. What sonar can't show is which cave systems and tunnel networks *happened* and which ones were *built*.

Survey Team RC8 were unlucky enough to make first contact with the Mole People.

They have a memory stone in Union Center now.

The Aghartan Drift is a sinkhole located at the base of a slanting lava tube lined with tunnel mouths like a cankered gullet. Beneath its pocked face lies an untapped aquifer of monumental proportions— this on Union say-so of course. This territory's belonged to the Mole People for far longer than anyone can surmise, yet here they are gunning on enemy turf. Union forces have surrounded the main Drift with a massive trench network supplemented by a web of watchtower outposts that actually go into the sinkhole itself, strapped to the gills with strung brass chimes that warn of approaching Moles.

Despite their efforts morale, supplies, and manpower have been slowly dwindling. The notorious Star-Nosed Prince, unseen in Subterran caves but ubiquitous on plastered propaganda, never seems troubled by things such as logistics and asset denial. The Mole People, less actual moles than bipedal cancer polyps, continue their inexorable slaughter.

The remaining soldiers of Subterranean 7th Heavy Rifles C-Group Blue sit in a trench dugout tunneled around halfway between their assigned posts. Nothing more than a parlor-sized wooden box choked with the pungent funk of warding incense and black coffee, a threadbare yellow lightbulb dangling from the middle of the ceiling. Mark IV Cleaver Corporal Chincoteague has broken down her organ gun and is running a wire brush through the bores. Conscripts Swann and Treeworth, the two halves of Dovetwin Tango, lay snuggled up in a single hammock with hats and rifles leaning against the wall.

The tape-player blares anew some doom metal, Chincoteague's pick. The room has a relaxed solemnity to it until footsteps come down the duckboards, jackboots of a Subterran officer with his sedge hat under one arm and behind him C-Group's Executive cleric, an incredibly unsettling humanoid called Chorba. The three vault to attention, a clatter as the wire brush falls to the floor.

"At ease. Looking for Corporal Chincoteague."

She steps forward. "Sir."

"Lieutenant Omar, 2nd Cannoneers. You're ranking here?"

"As of twenty-three-hundred, sir, barring the scriptures of your cleric."

"Walk with me a moment."

Distorted guitars shriek as they stride out into the trench, Chorba retreating inside the dugout to look for clothespins. Chincoteague runs one hand through her long raven mohawk, fluffs it out of its hat-induced flatness. The air is always chilly down beneath the wounded earth. In the no man's land between the sinkholes' sores soldiers are giving the dead and injured what they require, the sounds of shovels and the occasional crack of a revolver, technicians repairing cut chime wires.

"Leadership experience?"

"Chock full."

"Sarcasm?"

"Sir."

The Lieutenant stops and turns to face her. "We're kind of fucked right now, Corporal, let's be real. No one in the Union can pair fast enough to support this clusterfuck, no supply trolleys until the seventeenth. We're in a bad spot. I need to trust you to take care of your section basically on your own until we figure something out." He pauses. "That sounds like *shit* to say out loud."

"I'm primed like a fucking det-cord, Lieutenant. Are you asking me to extend 'preservation protocol' to others?"

"I am. You care they live or die, I assume."

"To the degree I ought. But that's their responsibility. I'm muscle."

"They're Tango, right?"

"They are."

"Then they're worth it. Let's try and keep the trenches out of Mole hands a little longer, keep your people alive. We'll get someone in as soon as someone's around."

"Sir."

Omar leaves her standing in the middle of the trench near the former watchtower, eyes glittering in the half-dark.

As the dusk hour commences, someone in the 7th Heavy gets their spotlight up and running for the first time in days and a beam of yellow cuts No Man's Land into buttered slices from a watchtower on the far side. The bioluminescent nerve endings of the Mole People really pop in a particular shade, glowing through the skin, and every wartime lamp, bulb, flare, and torch in Subterranean possession casts its light in this hue. A polyp can no longer infiltrate the municipal districts of Subterran lands undetected.

Chincoteague is in full Cleaver gear—sedge hat and armored fatigues of dark slate, black double-filter gas mask and bandoleer belt, trump card, black jackboots and plated gloves, her organ grinder (affectionately "Tomoe") across her knees, heavy service revolver at her belt, the great blade strapped across her back under the coat so that the haft juts out over her right shoulder. Her heart aches for a sortie. She sits in the trench cross-legged, eyes on the wall across, a few meters down from the dugout where she can hear Swann and Treeworth talking and kissing.

"Seal pie and slaw."

"What about pickled beets?"

"Part of the slaw. Don't want to crowd the plate."

"Whiskey?"

"Scotch?"

"I can work with that."

Smooch.

Chincoteague is a product of the Reintegrated Mark IV Michin Cleaver School, a Union program that sought to make the best of the remaining Subterranean excellence. Part training regimen part education system and part development laboratory, the R-IV sought to produce skilled heavy infantry with tenfold usefulness in the trenches. At the expense of some irreplaceable humanity, the battlemasters succeeded.

Victorious graduates were trained in preternatural use of war cleavers in close combat, five feet of terrible blued steel chopping weight.

They were trained to utilize exceptional situational awareness to assess the best possible circumstance for use of the trump card system.

They were trained to operate the five-barreled Chogun Foundry organ grinders, huge Gatling-type crank guns that fit into a special harness, allowing a Cleaver to advance while firing from the hip. Fed from .45-70 turn-key drums, Chincoteague must hand load match-grade ammunition into the hundred-capacity cans and clear the firing mechanism regularly to prevent jamming. The cartridges are unfortunately no longer manufactured, as years of Mole attrition has reduced the number of Cleaver graduates (primary caliber consumer) to a single digit number, but with precautions taken in its use it is a beast of a weapon.

"Quiet, thank fuck."

"Good thing she's out there."

"Good thing the lamp's up; see the Moles first."

Pause.

"I hear they eat their dead."

"I hear the Prince molds them from slugs, cultivates them."

Treeworth coughs. Irritated, Swann: "Are you laughing?"

"No!" Smooch. "No, something stuck in my throat. I don't know about that; I heard he captures Subterran citizens and turns *them* into Mole People."

"That's silly, though, no spies since the yellow. He'd have run out by now, after five goddamn years."

Smooch.

There's a long silence. Chincoteague watches a blanket of mist creep from the Drift, wonders what it must feel like to form that sort of attachment to someone. In her peripheral vision, the spotlight streaks and flashes. Presently she rises and meanders quietly down the duckboards to the foot of the watchtower, now a pile of burnt plywood. Somewhere underneath are the remains of the Sergeant. Chincoteague sits on a hunk of rock and studies the timbers. There's a white noise of murmurs and clattering from the sinkhole as those in the deep exchange information and mend chime wire.

"Dismember the third of September, eh?"

She turns to see Chorba standing with its hands in the pockets of its tunic, looking into the Drift.

"What's up, cleric?" Chincoteague is happy she can hide in the gas mask. "Didn't expect you around."

Chorba turns to her and smiles, its smooth hairless features bending upwards with no wrinkling of the flesh. Even Chincoteague's skin crawls. The cleric squats and gathers up a handful of rocky earth, inhales deeply of it. "Did you know talpidanthropy—belief in the existence of humanoid moles—was once a joke above ground, Cleaver?"

"Nope."

"One wonders if the Mole People are moles at all. Allegedly research has revealed they're rather like walking tumors."

"I heard something about that."

Chorba turns its gaping features to the ceiling of stone above. "I'm afraid it's likely true, Corporal. They are cancerous. Though my father gave me right and my mother left, I lost both in the wellwater."

"We'll excise the fuckers," the Corporal growls, staring into the Drift.

Chorba puts a hand over its eyes and bows, walking backwards. "Uh, goodnight, cleric."

"Keep an eye on the throat there, Corporal."

"Why's that?" But the cleric is already gone in the dark fog and mud. From somewhere in the sinkhole comes a dank exhalation of fetid air like a long sigh, some ancient pocket breached below.

Swann and Treeworth are now in their watchtower, making love by the flicker of candle flame. The Union recognizes the inherent and natural mystic power of deep love and orgasm, thus are couples suggested to join certain military positions and add their enigmatic energy to the fold. The True Jyori School of Knots trains lovers into Dovetwin units who fight past the point of mortal wounding at the death of their other and use mutual concentration to achieve vast feats of sex magic far more than the sum of the effort involved.

Dovetwin Tango being a relative crutch for this quadrant of trench, the two conscripted lovers have been given a decent amount of operational freedom.

The stilted platform here is one decked in dreamcatcher-like charms of Orgone accumulation, bark-and-iron amalgams like sexual lightning rods. The entwined figures shudder together, giving off a musky warmth in thrumming waves. If a Mole were to stick its face out of a hole nearby, it would see with its bizarre spectrum receptors a crimson halo of rolling tumbling spheres and pyramids and cubes spiraling around the watchtower, and it would feel fear, for a Mole cannot love.

Anointed incense roils out of the open watchtower, warding off polyps with its particular scent. Beneath the wooden struts, Chorba sits cross-legged, tunic tails splayed around it like white tentacles. Its red-rimmed lidless chicken eyes, yellow as the lanterns, dart between the four corners of the watchtower floor above. When it can hear them beginning to crescendo in sound and effort, the cleric gathers up a wad of mucus with such gusto its eyes roll into its head. Then laying back in the dirt, it heaves the blood-flecked gob up onto the underside of the watchtower. Smiling as they come together, the cleric rolls quietly away into the trenches.

They come over the wire then, the Moles, pale and stark in their tunnels.

The foremost ringer in the hole is slain before he can drag the bell but his arterial spray is seen by the next bellman up and he slings rope with force, the heavy chime network beginning to toll deep and mournful through the depths. A thick bolt catches the secondary in the chest and he staggers spitting blood. Dark eyes loom in force from the dark.

"MOOOOOOOOOOOLES!"

Fucking finally.

With neither hesitation nor second thought, Chincoteague vaults to her feet with a toothy grin, a dark hoplite bolting about the network ring of dugouts and tunnel-trenches. She can see incense smoke drifting from her squadmates' outpost and shrugs to herself, inhaling deeply through her nose and sighing at the crescendo of gunfire beginning to echo below. She shakes her head – really, how defenseless are they, fucking like rabbits up there – descends a duckboard plank over uneven rock down several meters to a lower level of more tunnelesque fortifications.

Lo and behold one of the goddamn Mole People crab-crawls

into her field of vision from a gap in the wood above used to thread bulb wire and straightens – two massive black eyes on a malformed and writhing white head, the wet black slit down the middle like a slicked vulva, a tongue of barbed wire lashing out at the air. It wears a high-collared white button-up shirt with a black string tie, black suspenders and black pants pinstriped over white spats on wingtips. At its waist dangles a hatchet with a carved wooden handle and an ornate head crusted with brown, tucked into a peculiar holster.

Chincoteague is unclipping the strap on Tomoe as the thing stands, letting her drop to firing position, and she sees the Mole grab for its hatchet not with its clawed-and-webbed digging talons, but with the six foot tongue of oxidized barbed wire that darts from its charcoal mouth. It whips the weapon from its holster as the Corporal grabs the handle of her gun and the crank and winds, the pre-primed drum feeding slugs down the chamber faster than a Mole can axe. With a twist of her arm *CHOOMCHOOMCHOOMCHOOM* the cancerous dandy disappears in a gushing vent of its own muddy black blood.

She runs then, hands on Tomoe and timing her ammunition usage as she moves down the tunnel. A dugout in the right of this ring connects to the sinkhole directly and three riflemen crouch here, Chogun bolt-actions beaded on the Drift as a clutch of Moles covered in human blood emerge piping and twining wire. The fire command goes out.

Chincoteague can't let Tomoe rip without hitting her countrymen and so she moves to support, her distance such that at least two of the Moles survive the rifle fire to butcher the Subterrans, hatchets lopping away as flesh is rent by claw. The Corporal winds the crank and a thunderous volley of .45-70s tear gelatinous white gobs from the remaining Moles, disintegrating bodies reeling onto the rotten plank floor as they fall apart from kinetic force. Chincoteague gives Tomoe a moment to cool herself, her senses awhirl with the adrenaline musk of a good fight, nary a thought for the comrades she's sworn to protect.

Swann feeds a cartridge into her rifle and closes the bolt. "Ammunition."

"Here."

A Mole slithers up the side of the Drift and out into no man's land proper, the mustard-colored spotlight making lines squirm across its face. She closes one eye and jams her tongue out the side of her mouth, exhales, misses it and hits the ground nearby, rock shrapnel chipping away. She curses and throws the bolt.

"Thermite grenade, babe, do something with this thing. I'm trying to focus."

Swann calls out the bomb and lobs it into the Drift. Treeworth caresses her bare thigh and she sighs, fires another round that joins the crackle and chatter of carbines around the sinkhole and blasts a Mole kneecap, if they have such things, out of its pants in an oily spray. The hatchet-wielding Mole polyps are beginning to chop, the sounds of wet thuds and whacks and yelps adding further darkness to the war symphony. Entwining his left leg over Swann's right, Treeworth hums a bass note she can feel through contact and they intone together,

"What have we that they have not
That lays our will so bare?
Worlds within our minds,
Life within our bodies,
Love within our hearts."

As the charms on the tower ceiling twinkle saffron in lamplight, the carmine shapes projected by the Dovetwin's unity begin rearranging themselves into a three-dimensional phalanx in the direction of the sinkhole, a shield of love to keep heartless Moles out.

A radio-operating Mole crouches on the lip of a tunnel mouth in the depths of the sinkhole. Such operators are distinguished by a coarse hooded jacket designed to cradle their communications bladder. It grabs the umbilical from its back and chirps into it in that curious piping Mole language, "See Baldermen forth—force casualty multiplies against heated metals and supershade lampcast."

Another group of brigands begins to trickle in amongst the hatcheteers, these clad in black jodhpurs and paddocks, string ties and burgundy waistcoats, a wooden contraption strapped to their back with a chest-crossing tangle of leather belts. Featuring a gear-

and-hinge loading system, the feeding mechanism attaches to a crossbow that can quite fairly be called a ballista. This is pulled over the Baldermen's shoulder with the right claw, the arm providing firing stability, the whole design intended to allow the ranged Mole mobility and freedom of talon to crawl and tear.

The Baldermen crawl out of the Drift and into the trenches. Nictitating membranes dart over icthyan optics as they send rusting quarrels of diseased metal whistling into Union bodies, spreading debilitating green-black veins of some unknown filth. Watchtowers open fire, thundering guns from dead wood gulches and the crimson devotion of Union spires against the terrible green poison and rusted axes of the Mole People.

Chincoteague vaults into a smoke-filled trench with one hand gripping the brace of her gun. Several Moles are crouched feeding on unfortunate Union fallen, whether dead or otherwise. Over their agonized chorus the Corporal reels up Tomoe braced against her hip as *BLAMBLAMBLAMBLAM* she pours slugs into the wood, the polyps, the dead, blood of all colors fountaining across the duckboard floor. Empty shell casings clatter against the wood, her face beneath the mask creased into a grin pale under the muzzle flash.

Dovetwin Tango are kneeling in the Watchtower, legs entwined and rifles propped on the sill, firing at the Baldermen who slither through the craters of no man's land. She is calmed by the touch of his skin— he, invigorated by the warmth of her proximity. This frustrates the everloving motherfuck out of the Moles, who see with their multi-field faculty a dense web of red geometrics not only disturbing to look at but that seem to attract Baldermen quarrels harmlessly away from the couple without ever visibly straying from place.

Two hatcheteers have formed a protection front for the Radio Mole, who's lost his assigned support team to a thermite blast. Polyps are busily keeping hot lead attention from the radio operator, which crouches with its broadcast bladder throbbing away. Spotting the pre-represented target, the Radio Mole gestures and the "squad" moves forwards, keeping low amongst the shredded corpses and puddles of muddy shrapnel and offal. Baldermen creep amongst the downed, executing wounded from either side, dragging some of the Moles away into the Drift. Rusting bolts weep bacteria into the soil.

"Olfactory plant confirmed."

They lay in the foul-smelling earth, yellow light casting squirming lines across their flesh, as the radio operator drags the umbilical up and lulls into its lamprey-like receiver, "Coordinate input prepared and guaranteed."

A nightmare drawl gurgles from the undulating acoustic membranes of the bladder. "Go for Central. Recall clearance from volatility locus."

"Go, Central. Ca-Set-Set-Ca-Lum-Eth turn grave Cha-Lum-Set-Lum-Tek."

"Locus narrowed. Widebeam received. Clearance. Clearance."

Dovetwin Tango are already sending a primed thermite grenade down, one which burns the two hatcheteers to death and scorches the radio operator. The message the Radio Mole sent is loud, clear, and successful however—thus a burning sphere of tumorous flesh, giving off a reek of burnt hair and something older comes roaring in an arc from the sinkhole mouth. At the edge of the barrier it breaks through with a sound like thunder and breaking glass, taking down the second watchtower in as many nights. Ruby hunks of shrapnel impale fleeing Moles; thick gases spill into the nearby dugouts and strangle Union soldiers with their own sore-covered tongues.

The Radio Mole, feeling the pale skin sluicing off its chest and face, flops out into the sinkhole, knocking askew some chimes as it tangles itself in wire. It flails to no avail, wriggling towards the black mouth of the Drift, pain drilling white needles into its face. A hand with no nails on the tips of its fingers darts from the darkness and grabs the radio operator around its peeling wrist. It squeals in a tone no human can hear as an equally rubbery face grins from the shadows.

"Found you."

Corporal Chincoteague makes her way back up into the wide field of trenches around the mouth of the Drift. She cranks Tomoe through the second-to-last third of her final slugcan, *BLAMBLAMBLAMBLAM* fleeing Mole bodies breaking apart like rotted gourds spurting a sluggish ichor. The ground around the duckboards squelches underfoot with multiple bloods. As another succession of those vile artillery rounds vomit from the sinkhole like the flaming contents of a public bathroom drain, Chincoteague sights herself a convenient dugout and strafes across its threshold. In its amber belly a line of cots bear moaning soldiers by the fizzling light of electric torches. Nurses move amongst the wounded as the wooden roof of the hovel creaks ominously under the ghastly assault of target-seeking Mole howitzers.

The Corporal ambles amongst the beds, buckles her gun back up to the right side of her chest, leans away from the heat wavering off the barrels. She excuses herself around the nurses, who part for her with terrified eyes, a faceless black totem smoking with alien blood and burnt metal. She's about to exit the ambulance vault when a bloodied hand shoots from beneath a sheet and grabs a tail of her campaign coat, yanks hard enough to get her attention. She turns the lensed sockets of her gas mask to the stained cloth figure below.

"Cleaver."

Chincoteague lowers herself to one knee. The figure scowls.

"What's your unit?"

"C Blue, sir."

"Chincoteague."

The Corporal bristles. "Excuse me?"

The bandaged frame on the cot tears the gauze from its head. A series of massive gas sores have taken up the right half of Lieutenant Omar's face, pocked craters of flesh weeping translucent pus. His eye is a red line hidden beneath the bloated yellow surface of its own infected lid. Omar grabs her coat by its thick lapel and yanks her down close with dead man's strength, rasping into her face, "Ground zero chemical contact attempting to gather support for a love-pair barely holding this sector of the Drift together. You loose fucking cannon." He coughs a red string of spit down his chest.

Chincoteague stands there a few moments longer but Omar says nothing more, only hacks himself into fitful unconsciousness. She nudges his shoulder gently with the back of one gloved hand. Then she departs the field hospital, nurses avoiding her path, the smell of blood filling the filters of her mask.

The cleric is kneeling in the dugout before an Executive idol, whispering into its cupped hands. A fist-sized cone of consecrated incense smolders on the floor. Corporal Chincoteague kneels down quietly next to Chorba as it prays and waits. Presently the ascetic ceases whispering and, without moving its eyes, turns its head to face her. "Yes?"

"I, uh...I'm not sure what to do."

The cleric cocks its head.

"I'm not religious, but we're a little low on help, huh?"

Still Chorba says nothing, just stares unblinking, fists a closed tube in front of its mouth.

"Pretty much lost the squad. Think there's a decent chance that cannoneer Lieutenant wired in a court marshal. I have no way of knowing, but...it's certainly not out of the question."

"Union intent? What Executive will does your development enforce?" Chorba drops its hands and Chincoteague sees that for some reason its chewed its own lips nearly to shreds.

Staring at the cone of incense, the Corporal begins to slowly rock back and forth on her knees.

"I'm a weapon."

"I choose to aid in the execution of your purpose. I trust you're not yet the last."

"No." She stares at it for a long moment. "I think the 9th Heavy Marksmen and another cannoneer unit house the remaining graduates. They haven't come to a point where they've decided trump system usage is the most expeditious available enterprise. They still support their squads, last I understood."

Chorba smiles and Chincoteague's spine crawls. "We'll work quickly and quietly to make the violence happen. I have a gift for us." It retreats to the shadows of the dugout and re-emerges bearing the severed head of a Mole, its black mouth sagging agape, a bizarre balloon-like object dangling from the base of the neck. A long fleshy tube wraps around the throat and ends near the mouth.

Chorba proffers the decapitated polyp. "It sings in yellow light. An auditory key of some sort, based on the musical nature of their broadcast language. Remember them and I'll get you into the sinkhole where you can die a warrior's death."

Chincoteague stares into the equally vacant eyes of the dead

Mole, an inch of barbed wire sliding out of the slack vertical lips with a liquid sigh.

The chime wardens, eyes darting nervously about, mutter begrudging assent and begin lowering Chincoteague into the sinkhole with lengths of spare bellwire.

"Shit!"

The line slackens as the Corporal slams into the sinkhole wall. She grabs hold of a protrusion and, hands sliding, watches the wire length fall into the dark below. As it gathers speed she braces her legs in a crouch against the earthen wall and shoves off, the momentum of the falling cable hurtling her deep into the abyss.

Wind whistles around the sockets of the gasmask as the fall lengthens to a point she doubts she'll survive. *I guess it was worth a shot.* Even as the thought whispers in her ear, she smashes hard on her back into something thickly textured. She begins sinking into the mystery cushion and so rolls to her feet, switching on a yellow electric hip torch.

Horror—a pile of human and Mole corpses, careless combat casualty tosses and accidental slip-and-falls both, she assumes. She staggers back, her campaign coat heavy with multiple bloods, shrugs it off her shoulders and sights a wooden portal fastened to a rough cave opening with large iron hinges. She gives this door a solid push and follows the tube it reveals.

The serpentine corridor is lit periodically by oil lanterns that flash battalions of leaping shadow down the grotto walls. A rotting carpet of faded burgundy covers the length of the floor. The Corporal begins to hear an increasingly unnerving sound at increasingly frequent intervals, the sound of someone trying to run a broken motor, the sound of a fanbelt tearing itself to shreds, the sound of a factory manipulator plunging itself into a vat of smelted ore—a harsh industrial shriek.

The tunnel opens onto a vast underground gorge with long folds of fat chainmail hanging from the ceiling, a black pit below. The walls of this chasm are carved into windows and doors, rock homes long since abandoned—Chincoteague can see puddles of melted wax on sills, shattered pottery shadowed by chiseled thresholds. The top quarter of the chasm is encircled by ancient oil lanterns, some dead, some nearly falling from their mounts, some simply bare hooks.

Criss-crossing the cave roof's mail is a system of sagging cables leading to and from the various mouths of old homes and other connecting caves. Chincoteague sees at least three portals across the gap lit by fresh oil. White that could be bone litters their thresholds.

The fat links are a catch-all for heavy hooks. Unlatching a pair and spacing her weight between her arms, the Corporal slides precariously across the hole as machine wails echo from its flickering depths. She slams bodily into the floor of the roof-most fracture and is taken aback by what appears to be a Mole field hospital at the end of the worn hall—she sees cots and kerosene lamps, at least.

The field ambulance is a short L-shape with a sigil-covered duckboard roof and a floor of petrified slop. The leg she walks down is unpopulated but as she turns into the short angle the last few beds are occupied. She catches sight of a top-hatted figure latching the far door behind it and then she's locked in.

The patients are wrapped head to toe in concertina wire rusting with dark blossoms of dried blood. Buckled to their beds with fraying leather straps, quiet but painful groans issue from bizarre places beneath the metal casts. All three are hooked up to IV drips filled with black Mole fluids, but one is also secured to an amber jar the Corporal decides is either radiolarian or filthy, given the wriggling shapes that dart within.

A sweating Chincoteague winds up the last third of her organ grinder and chews two of the wired bodies to bits, tearing through their bodies and beds with oily geysers of chunky blood. She pulls the barrels apart and grabs a handful of the firing mechanism with her fist, yanks it out in an almost-comical blast of springs and gears. "Sorry, my love." She offers a bonus prayer to Chogun Foundry. Can't have the Moles figuring *that* thing out, though, fuck. She pulls her heavy caliber service revolver from its belt holster and plants a bullet in the head of the remaining patient before she begins to kick at the latch of the exit.

With no warning whatsoever the door slams inwards heaving

her to the floor on her back in a heap.

Without further steadying she trains her pistol on the door.

Nothing fills the frame.

Then a top hat, which disappears as she opens fire, pops the cylinder and slides home her last six rounds, the hat's owner in the door then on the floor then laying on a cot then holding her arms against the duckboards. It's a Mole with no eyes, dirty mesh screens poorly sutured over the sockets, its barbed wire tongue whipping against her mask carving furrows into the lenses. She struggles against its clawed grip, throws her weight around as it splits its vertical mouth into a screeching hole wider than she's seen a Mole make, a wet black horror churning and grinding with flaking wire filaments.

She bunches her knees up and kicks the thing off her, which proves to be a mistake as it grabs for and levels a weapon on the ground next to it. It looks like an old school blunderbuss with a hollow skeleton stock and the reel mechanism of an old film projector mounted on the top of the receiver. Chincoteague sees a double-stacked hammer designed to hit the ribbon around the reels at the same time it strikes the flint of the lock.

With a squeeze the aberrant musket screams an interplanal succession of disintegrating silver ghosts at the Corporal, whispering howling truths, an avalanche of unlight cast from umbral stars crashing down on the good Corporal in a laughing conga line of rotting top hats. Accordion music blended with the burning screams of dying families assaults her ears and she seizes on the floor in a puddle of her own urine, a trickle of blood from one nostril, saliva congealing in thick gobs at the corners of her mouth as the closing latch of the Mole hospital echoes in a lost space against her head.

Crimson and silver flicker against her eyelids.

Dry tongue dredging across cracked lips.

Somewhere, someone is crying.

She reaches high above her chest with one shaking palm, and after a deep sigh that seems to come from far further back than this moment, slams the hand down.

VICTORY

She vaults upright arms jerking wildly, legs trembling and knees buckling in a seizing wind-up dance, knocks over two or three cots and an oil lantern and sets the canvas quietly aflame behind her.

With the selfsame shaking hand she tears off the scuffed gas mask.

Tears off the ragged sedge hat, the black gloss of her mohawk pressed flat against one side of her head.

Tears off the fatigue tunic to reveal the dragline spider-fiber undershirt she wears smoking with the silver filaments and black exhaust of the Mole's gunblast, the most prominent feature the x-shaped leather-steel-and-plastic harness buckled across her back and attached to a grey box stapled cruelly to the flesh between her breasts. The straps on the front side of her body hold three soft red squares each for a total of twelve, the squares triple wired to the box. The unit holds, in addition to a digital timer screen with knob and a bare rat's nest of zip-tied wire connectors, a large red button and a large blue button.

The red button has been depressed.

When well-intentioned and well-trained Cleaver Corporal Minjae Chincoteague slammed home the first activator of her system, she injected her heart directly with an experimental combat stimulant dubbed PhubelX9. PX9 could be compared to a modified adrenaline rush the way drinking espresso could be compared to eating a pile of candy. This is to say that Corporal Minjae Chincoteague has ceased to exist. May her next of kin if there be any know of her courage. She has died in battle.

The woman rocking slowly back and forth on the Mole People field ambulance floor is the fifth Cleaver of her graduating class, Cleaver V, V for VICTORY.

The woman staggers to her feet. Revolver forgotten, she undoes the final buckle of her harness – grabs the three foot haft on her back with the fireaxe-style crooked end wrapped in gauze and masking tape. Two feet longer atop this handle are taken by a two-foot-wide, inch-thick piece of blued steel tapered to a gleaming edge and engraved with disruptive anti-neoplastic equations of sub-molecular Executive assent.

A wooden door really stands no chance against the war cleaver of Victory Five.

The Moles are seeing a face with which humanity was seldom graced, though no longer in its original china-doll condition. Deep ice-colored eyes that once glanced somewhat coyly down a slenderly tapering nose have been turned nearly black by overwhelmed pupil, the sclera red with popped capillaries. The mischievous grin of charmingly crooked teeth is now stained with the blood leaking from her gums. The mohawk lays in shining waves down the left side of her head and neck, the exposed shaven skin bulging with overworked veins.

Hatcheteers are holed up in the next hallway, what appears to be a long line of individual recuperation cells. The occupied rooms she passes all feature bare wire beds and ravenous polyps attempting to consume prisoners of war with their gaping vaginal jaws. These unsuspecting gourmands meet the business end of the sprinting Cleaver's war blade. She's breathing fast enough to call it hyperventilating, a necessity to keep up with her now vastly accelerated metabolism. The nutrients in PX9 should keep her going for just a little longer.

Chop. Chop. Remember to breathe. Chop. I can smell your blood.

She laugh/exhales a mist of red out of her mouth, then can't stop laughing, the husky guffaw gaining volume until a coven of Baldermen drilling in the barracks are brought to alarm attention. The hatcheteers in their bunk cells shrink from her alien baying. The blood-spraying howl of the human loose in the Mole People's fortress is the most alarming sound they've ever heard.

A hatcheteer reels from a doorway, talons swiping, eyes bugged out. It whips its hatchet at Victory Five in a three-foot arc and she bends back like limbo, swings the cleaver low to the right with one arm, takes the Mole's left leg out from underneath. It falls squealing to the floor in a black puddle and she lops its head off with a mirthful heave.

As the cleaving edge meets the flesh of a Mole, the symbols carved upon it flare with intent and part the viral tissue beneath in a rapidly-decomposing torrent.

Three more hatchet-wielders fall to her blade—one with a diagonal pie slice missing from its left shoulder down – one she catches in the air as it leaps towards her, meets its torso with the edge of the cleaver and brings it smashing to the ground in two halves—

the last dies with its wire tongue held fast in her off hand, slamming the blunt top edge of the cleaver down on its face again and again until the wire tears from its jaw and the eyes have ruptured, the crooked white face caving into a tar-colored puddle.

The Cleaver crumples to her knees as she exits the feeding bunks into what at first seems to be some sort of amphitheater. A moment's heavily drugged consideration reveals rather an inverted ziggurat, massive stone or carven steps descending down to a structure in the very center. The cave is dark except for the dim orange light that descends from a ceiling chimney and the ancient oil lanterns ringing the central building. Victory Five likens it to an overexaggerated baroque carriage—all dark metal with Rococo wrought hooks and leering faces. It's about two stories high, the outside lined with dark stained wood and burgundy leather, copper accents long gone green.

The upended ziggurat with the carriage center is silent but for the miniscule lappings of lantern flame.

The PX9 has pretty much taken its toll. Coughing up a rope of red, the Cleaver leans back and slaps the blue button on her chest as a tremor runs down the length of her body. Staggering uneasily to her feet she inhales through her nose and out through her mouth, letting Chiroptic Batch Delta mix with PX9 and pickle her blood, buying her additional focus and time to set off her vest. The entirety of her eyes and gums flood tar-black. Blood leaks from her nose and ears, beads where her teeth meet.

The door of the carriage house flings open.

The Mole with the eye-screens and the ratty top hat stands there, musket hanging causally at its side, as it peers about the temple. When it sees Victory Five rocking and chuckling and bleeding with a Mole-gory cleaver at her side, it screams words. With its foreign jaw and lip structure, the vocal sound is that of a panflute of human bones.

The screaming is in English.

"SORCERER! Fucking *SORCERER!*" The Mole raises its gun and hurtles another salvo of unsilver wailing moon-shadows – this time Victory's cleaver cuts the faces of luminescent singularity to shrieking ribbons. The Mole, still yelping that she's some sort of witch, turns to exit through the carriage door again and she hurls the blade with all her might, catching it in the spine, splitting its forest-green trenchcoat through to the pale flesh and black blood of its back. The gunmole writhes there on the floor, moaning in assumed pain in its unsettling warble.

The Cleaver reaches to the back of her belt as she strides down the stone steps and removes the half-burnt cassette player strapped there. Flicking the on switch several times, she fiddles with both knobs before an *aha* moment. She places one boot on the back of the dying Mole's knee and jacks the volume as low-pitch guitars begin to wail.

"Oh!" Victory Five makes a mock surprised face, and the arched eyebrows over the black eyes and gums, the blood leaking from her orifices, is almost scarier than any mannequin smile. "This is a particularly good one."

She yanks the cleaver from the Mole's leaking spine and slams it down once. An ornate elliptical seal over the elevator doors within the carriage would intimidate her if she couldn't see several pipes within. Dimming the radio she yanks the handle that dangles like a door knocker and with a puff of dust the door system tweets out a tune. From the depths of her stimulant-addled consciousness she reaches with a dusky blue claw and grabs the broadcast bladder's return clearance code from churning memory.

She purses her lips and gives a raspy red spray.

Shit focus fuck focus focus tune what was the yellow tune kill it if you can

She whistles the notes on her third try, lips slick with blood.

With an eerie little calliope-note confirmation, the doors part horizontally.

From there it's a straight shot down. If she wasn't blaring metal and having a serious tweak fit, the Cleaver would see some things not meant for human eyes through the tiny portholes and worn gaps in the cave wall during descent.

A massive cocoon throbbing with dozens of white lobes that glow from within.

A triple rack of naval-style cannons the size of factory exhaust pipes lit by floodlight.

A gyrating grid of wire fence cages and leather belts stuffed with naked human beings in various states of dismemberment and decomposition, gangrenous IV drips gathered at the center and looped across to every occupant, the entire mess dangling over light that flickers like an open flame.

A chittering three-foot Mole in a lantern-filled tunnel, a massive yellow tusk jutting one each from the top and bottom of its vertical mouth, a shovel in its claws.

Even—yes—a glittering sapphire lake, a vast stone chalice shimmering with jeweled light.

A third song is underway when the elevator vomits Victory Five into a heavily be-lanterned staircase, a descent both sharp and narrow carpeted in fraying royal blue. As the decline becomes deeper cables and copper pipes begin to line the ceiling, the nest growing more elaborate with miniature boilers and pressure protectors. The tunnel opens into a wide oval with a floor and walls of filthy ceramic tile, metal catwalks and a railed balcony above, an enormous flaming crystal chandelier dangling at the far end.

In the very middle, ringed by chains and pulleys and cables and catwalks and ray-tube computers and conveyors is something like a hundred-foot-tall flexile sea anemone of pale decaying flesh, a cratered bruise-colored tube with a crown of six enormous human-looking fingers that stretch towards the chimney-hole carved bordering the chandelier above. Electrodes and IV drips surround an oven door set into the side of the thing—the out-of-place medical equipment connects to a coat-rack like arrangement of the same bladders found on the Radio Mole, these linked to a thick antenna twined with oil-slick blue umbilical cords. The Cleaver can see a boiler fire burning within the monster as well as three slender black tentacles of varied declining fettle set in gaunt depressions in the tissue. These follow the terrible bloody figure that approaches them, a suffering revenant emaciated from the untested toxin cocktail eating away within.

A great piping, a foghorn tone with alternating notes, fills the cave from the mouth of the thing. From deep inside the boiler flame comes a voice, several layered pitches with a rasping mechanical tone. The voice is the uncooled engine running itself to burnout, the steam press that's killed a worker, the tree shredder devouring the heedless schoolchild.

"CLARITY BLACK," it shrieks in Mole. "INFILTRATOR IN THE SUPPRESSION WARD."

Cleaver Victory Five sways forwards, the blade at her side dragging sheets of sparks off the catwalk. The balcony has silently filled with Baldermen, ballistae readied, the ground floor with Moles in the doorways, hatchets whipping around their faces. At the forefront of the hatcheteers stands a Mole in a capotain and navy blue waistcoat, one of the blunderbuss film projectors held across its stomach. A pair of enormous transparent dragonfly wings, the veins shot through with black, jut folded from its spinal column.

The Suppressor speaks in disturbingly clear English, that same mind-shattering tone. "KILLING FOR WATER OR BLOOD?"

Victory Five gives it a drunken bloody smile and, after dredging her addled mind for the words, lisps in a crimson spray, "Just doing my job. You're killing *us*."

"YOU RAID OUR LANDS, SUN-LOVER. THESE WATERS ARE OUR WATERS. NO NEGOTIATION."

She shrugs and grins. "I bear a sword, not a suitcase."

"KILL HER."

Full headway into the metal by now as the tortured banshee of former Corporal Chincoteague howls at the top of her lungs, an ear-splitting shriek as she swings the war cleaver and dashes hatcheteers to oily chunks, the slices they manage to axe into her exposed skin not doing much to slow her.

She rolls beneath the epileptic antiwave blasts of the head Mole's musket and cripples it, fires its own terrible weapon into its gasping mouth until black foam squirts from around the eyes and they dangle on nerve endings against its alabaster cheeks.

She grabs the barbed wire of a hatcheteer to drag it close and hacks away at its torso, the morpheme-amplified cleaver edge rotting away flesh in shuddering layers as it brutalizes the tissue below.

She dices a single polyp into several indistinguishable hunks of raw tissue.

As she thins out the hatchet-wielders the final issue comes into focus—the Baldermen. There are a lot of fucking Baldermen on that balcony up there and they have a much clearer firing field now that the risk of striking their fellows has more than halved. A hail of whistling bolts thunk into the tiles and catwalks beneath her as the Suppressor begins to scream—the cacodaemonic industrial howl that's been echoing has been the sound of this horrid pillar gathering energy.

Flames lick from the oven door.

The IV drips throb an infected orange.

The antenna crackles with black lightning as the fingers buckle and fling a scorched globe of melting decay up the chimney.

As Baldermen bolts begin to penetrate her exposed skin, blackening her already weakened limbs, Cleaver Victory Five knows the PX9 and CBD have done their utmost. She twists the knob atop her trump card system. The digital timer on the front gives a countdown of ten seconds before the dozen shaped charges on her chest detonate with the force of 5,000 tons of trinitrotoluene. Amidst volleys of bolts she limp-drags herself to the foot of the vomiting, screaming Suppressor and flips it the bird.

Then they're all burning, flesh charring to ashen husks in the roaring cyclone her body unleashes.

A certain Executive cleric convulses with fitful gasps in the tunnels far above, hands clasped, singing as the ground beneath it trembles in lamentation.

FULL
FATHOM
FIVE

What's the worst that could happen?

The tank's motor grinds up to bear and begins its inexorable sluggish crawl past perimeter post and outer wire. Notched iron treads kick dusky plumes of ashen salt, the siege engine's ploughblade dangling a foot above grey rock. A storm roils in the cloudless sky above as the *Banks of Eurotas* pours over-amped chemical lightning onto the Reef's champion, the shrieking war-titan leaking tumors as it lurches puppeted by the toxic oceans of a polluted Earth, a man-made horror born of endless war and a species' ignorance.

The crew sit with worn pieces of human femur across their knees, distanced from the camaraderie of the other tankers. With a shaking left hand short one pinky the commander holds a steaming plastic flask of coffee no more than black water. They performed the Rite of Expulsion together a week ago—there's still a faded handprint of human blood flaking from their faces. They've only consumed water that's gone through the process of purification—boiling, mantras, boiling, incense, boiling. Draining. Filtering. No solid food.

A hundred years earlier, Agent Cold Snap—given name Isaac Bennett—can smell the tangy, salty stink of polluted shoreline as soon as he enters town. It's a little foggy, a little muggy, a little toasty for late March, and people are taking advantage of the unseasonable warmth to eat at outdoor cafes or walk their pets. Women in sport clothing, men in gym shorts, tiny dogs wearing stupid little t-shirts.

Bennett makes for the antibiotic dead drop, prescription telegraphed in the prior evening by the Operator back at Five of Cups. Mom-and-pop pharmacy, no pseudomedical poison here just the over-the-counter classics. He asks the clerk about the weather as they pass a white paper bag, gets no conclusive answer.

In a small arboretum he swabs his inner elbow and mainlines the syringe, rigorously coded prophylactics rushing into his bloodstream.

A blonde woman comes jogging by, hair swaying against her shoulder blades, an mp3 player strapped to her upper arm.

"Excuse me, miss..."

"Kent."

"Miss Kent, I'm Roger Waters, with the National Weather Service. You notice anything weird around town lately, uh pertaining to the weather, sudden temperature or pressure changes? Odd coloration? Besides the obvious." During darker times a decade gone, some zealot detonated a chemical bomb the size of a Volkswagen Beetle in the middle of Springfield and the sunsets have never been the same.

The woman apologizes, shakes her head and continues along the path. Bennett feels his top shirt button's come undone, hurriedly reclasps it. No wonder she bolted, probably saw a web of bruise coming off his chest.

A shock of electricity between his temples —itinerary downloading. *WHITE BOY FOUR O'CLOCK PM COORDINATES IN BOARD REEF INTRUSION 94.4 PERCENT LIKELY*

He checks into the motor lodge early, takes his shoes off, smokes an inkstick and pops the television on. Scanning channels he catches snippets of warnings, water toxicity elevated, caution on shorelines, a rash of bombings. Channel 23 strobes a series of numbers through the static, coordinates he might not've seen if it weren't for the company unguent riding his arteries.

Bennett heads North after a brief nap. In one of the forests that smear the New Hampshire-Massachusetts border, he runs into a long-haired man in a black suit whose shoes and pantlegs are clogged with mud. Within the trees Bennett can hear something whispering, a thick and slimy sound.

The man turns, hand on the huge grips of a thigh-holstered pistol. "Cold Snap?"

"Yeah. You White Boy?"

"One and only. Show me."

Bennett unbuttons the top of his shirt to show the bruising around his consumption cross, the Tarrare Implant, his personal devil and reason for service. White Boy nods. "That's it. Got yours on accident, huh?"

Bennett coughs. "No word from the Tannhauser boys?"

"All cozy in a vault in Geneva, not taking their chances here."

"I thought I was meeting Snake Eyes."

"And I thought you were bringing Amanda the Man-Cutter with you."

Bennett shakes his head.

White Boy stares down at his shoes. "I don't like all these last minute changes."

"We've been scrambling at every Reef ping." Bennett steps down the embankment into the treeline. "Attican couldn't light her candles fast enough. Lost a Golgotha just trying to zip me out. She's going fucking crazy back there."

"She knows it's getting bad."

"Is it?"

"You'll see. You have any bones on you?"

"Not my gig, sorry."

They walk ahead about ten meters before Bennett takes a booth down one end of the diner next to an open window. As far as the current state of the world, there's no better place in a hundred miles to get a better burger. He orders it draped with the works and still mooing to boot, settles in with a root beer and braces his back in the corner where he can relax but still see the door.

He'll have to get used to eating with his mouth out here, not his chest. Tarrare Implants aren't exactly commonplace and he'd likely be driven stoned from town by a peasant mob. He shouldn't need to eat anything here he'd normally use the Implant for, anyway, like drone missiles or bomb vests.

A blonde woman comes jogging by, hair swaying against her shoulder blades, an mp3 player strapped to her upper arm. "I would give my left testicle for a fucking flamethrower, bud." She flicks a snail from her thigh.

Bennett starts stuttering. "Uh, Miss Kent, uh—seen anything weird, uh—any earthquakes around here? We're just trying to figure out if there's anything to worry about."

Miss Jordan Kent—who's drowned seven neighborhood cats, countless squirrels, and the only child she ever birthed in the very tub in which she washes herself weekday mornings – smiles a socially-acceptable smile that doesn't quite reach her eyes. The flesh of the diner patrons' faces stretches as if pulled from the back, the bone visible in the gaps of their skulls black and pitted. Water rushes from the nearest drainage grate and the street begins to flood. The cook turns as the skin sags off his face in a gush of dingy water and shuffles forward.

"No, no, *NO!*" echoes the century back at Five of Cups, where Operator Attican stands surrounded by chanting Golgotha flickering with transient candlelight. She yanks a lever on the nearest console. "Stabilize, stabilize *NOW!*"

"Sorry, ma'am!" yelps a nearby attendant. "They're coming on strong up in Mass! Our boys must be close!" He slides a tongue of punchcard into his desk and it regurgitates. He slides it in again and then a third time. The walls tremble as if hit with artillery.

"Somebody bring this whole goddamned shithouse back in order! MARS doesn't drop to the fucking Reef! I want reactive anti-colossal measures engaged and word to standby units to bring everything to bear. Do not let that shell hit!" She shakes her Siouxsie Sioux hair, wipes the sweat from her palms. Around her, the Golgotha moan and shiver and twitch, flailing one arm spasmodically in the air above their heads, impossibly fast as if the joints are on jerking strings.

"This is insane!" screams another attendant, raking his fingernails down his face. "It's already happened! It's going to happen! *You can't*—" a hole opens in his head, most of the matter within decorating his console.

Attican slides her .38 back into her coat pocket. "The Reef *will not* enter this worldline. I don't care how unstable we are and I don't care about inevitability. If we stop the slug, we stop the loop.

Are we clear?"

The other attendants nod. "I'd have done the same, ma'am."

"We're with you."

Ladies and gentlemen, we're experiencing a Stage Five Transgressive Event. If you would kindly place all electronics in the garbage disposal and tune your televisions to channel twelve, further bulletins will issue as events warrant. Thank you for your attention.

White Boy falls backwards into the silvery rays of an undersea sunrise. With a determined sniff he breaks open his Thompson Contender and slides in a fluorescent yellow .45-70 Reality Cracker, takes aim across his forearm and blasts the waterlogged star into a burst of molten newspaper clippings, a smell of burning nitrous and old leather.

Somebody or something screams, an agonized sound.

White Boy opens a briefcase and tosses a pair of goggles to Bennett, thick aviation-looking suckers with wires and diodes and shit strapped to the outside. "Fabric distortion up ahead. If that's not a clear indicator...the area gets swampy, floral decomposition. Chronoplastic residue."

In the night there's a sudden sound in his home—he shoots from bed with the practiced defensiveness of an active-duty combatant and frog-walks onto the landing, a hunter's knife like the tooth of some deceased metal predator gleaming in his right hand. Somewhere one of the radiators is leaking and a soft hissing whine fills the first floor of the house.

"I promise you want to get the fuck out of my house, whoever you are."

A figure soaked to the bone in a torn pullover sways drunkenly at the foot of the stairs and jerks their head to the open front door, as if someone behind them just called their name.

That distress beacon beneath the Montauk Lighthouse, enough blood to fill a Three Mile cooling tower but not a single fucking corpse to boot? Remember how the place looked untouched for decades though we'd been there six months before? We just turned off the beacon and left.

The satchel's been rummaged but a cursory inspection tells Operator Attican everything's in there. Probably just wanted to wave fumigation lanterns around the bag. Whatever the townspeople below are coming down with, it catches quickly.

Three scrolls of tattered parchment, two fountain pens.

A chisel, a mallet, a stag-hilt dagger.

Three scraped and bleached human femurs.

"Osteomancy's no bullshit."

Bennett descends to Subdistrict C. The encroaching wetlands, once just a heavily shunned pond, begin to burble between mangrove trees, shimmering with oilslick rainbows. Down in the swamp, beneath the cover of the treetops where no sane person would ever tread, echoes the unmistakable shuffling sound of something sloshing through the water.

Above Five of Cups, halls of long-decayed tile connect square pits and stairwells spiralling down through layers and layers of stores and kiosks and shops and boutiques. All closed and shuttered grey, but bright neon reds and blues and yellows flicker and buzz still, echoing with droplets of water. At the bottom Operator Attican closes the bulkhead with a submarine-style door lock.

Ladies and gentlemen, the Metahazard Assault Response Service has issued Transgressive activation warnings to prevent accumulating chronoplastic shutdown. If you would kindly remove all canine teeth from yours and your children's mouths, if applicable, and tune your televisions to channel sixty-four, further bulletins will issue as events warrant. Thank you for your attention.

The Tarrare Implant in Bennett's chest goes haywire and his ribcage opens up like the legs of a crab, clamps down around the steering wheel. The Caprice goes careening up off the side of I-90 and down a rapid incline towards a concrete drainage pipe. He grasps the interior for dear life as glass shatters and metal bends, the car crumpling like a paper cup. His ribcage begins chewing its way out of the wreckage as he nurses a broken arm and a nosebleed.

Must be two in the morning when he gasps awake drenched in sweat, grabbing at nothing.

Standing to stretch he turns as an unexpected breeze cools his clammy midriff, bruised and bloody, criss-crossed with surgical sutures.

The window is open just a crack.

Willing himself to remember whether or not he opened it before bed, Bennett has to admit he's ultimately the most likely culprit, given the calm chill of recent nights and his inability to recall what he even ate for lunch the same day anyways.

Pulling it closed he hears a ringing note, sort of a wind chime sound. He re-opens the window against his better judgment and that familiar creeping heat begins to mount his throat as he hears a number of notes. Not a wind chime but singing of some kind, a soft dissonant moaning.

It sounds like it's coming from right beneath his window but when he leans and looks, nothing's below and suddenly the sound seems to be coming from the bordering trees. Then the crunching shriek of some small animal meeting a violent death.

Smell of saltwater, stagnant, cloying.

Smell of the Reef.

In an alley somewhere a dog barks.

The jukebox in the corner is blown out, a few stray specks of blood on the shattered front.

From nowhere a dish of the special slides in front of him and he chows down, the air thick with the smells of garlic and oil and spilled alcohol. Eventually the bartender makes her way over, wipes her hands and grimaces stained silver. "What do you want?"

"You still roll nerve gas?"

"No." She rubs her hand sideways on the bartop. *Usual room.*

"You still have a lavatory on the premises?"

"As always."

Bennett takes the faded red velvet stairs three at a time. Up here are storage closets and bathrooms, a few unused bedrooms repurposed for god knows what. In the mens' room, mercifully empty, the last toilet stall of the three with the dented lever – off with the top of the tank and as always, the key to Storeroom D on the end of the hall.

The door's locked, of course. He uses the key and there the bartender is, sitting on the end of a crate of malt liquor, sawed-off across her lap. It's a positron conversion, cables and compensators pulsing with violet light, duct tape wrapped around the beaten wood foregrip to keep it attached. The barrels are not quite pointing in his direction.

"It's the Reef. It's always the Reef. Always has been, always will be. Fix your oceans, mate."

Ladies and gentlemen, we've received confirmation that MARS associates will be deploying to no less than seven cities across the Central States. If you would kindly keep at least fifty feet from all water sources and tune your televisions to channel ninety-three, further bulletins will issue as events warrant. Thank you for your attention.

The tank has a single chronoplasmic slug loaded—the crew's been ordered to defer from all engagement excluding their single target, the horrible old waterlogged war-titan, a corpse dominated by the Reef. The idea is simple—send the monstrosity, by proxy the Reef's consciousness, into a waterless future under a dying red sun.

A man with no eyes in his sockets save pitted black coral leaps atop a ruined car wailing in whalesong and lifts his thumb to the air. With a *CRACK* he disappears in a haze of black fragments and brackish water. In the cockpit the driver, voice warped by fear, screams, "No temporal imprint!"

There's the sound of a clock's internal mechanisms, deafening loud, and the crew's vision goes a blurry red as blood pours from nostrils. The ritual incisions across the backs of hands open and weep anew. From a great distance comes a woman's roar of frustrated anger.

"Holy shit, if we don't get this under control we are well and truly fucked," mutters Attican to no one in particular, runs a manicured hand through her hair.

The candle has gone out inside one of the Golgotha's heads and she whips out a Zippo and relights it. At least half of her attendants are dead at their consoles, blood leaking from facial orifices. She fiddles with a set of chrome knobs on one, yanks two levers on another, punches in green codewords that raster across black screens.

The window tub in weekday mornings smiles a socially-acceptable flamethrower. She flicks a snail that doesn't quite reach her eyes. Flesh stretches from bone visible in a crack. Willing to remember a man with no eyes opened it before his inability to recall a ringing note, sort of against his better judgment and dissonant moaning heat as singing of some kind.

The crunching shriek of some violent crew with worn pieces of knees distanced from the camaraderie. With a short pinky the commander holds no water. The Rite of Expulsion – a faded handprint gone through no food and shit strapped to the outside.

"Fabric decomposition residue."

There the clock's deafening vision pours. White Boy opens his briefcase and comes jogging by, hair swaying against thick suckers. The ritual incisions weep from a great distance. Darker times detonated a woman's roar of frustrated anger. Two in the morning when he gasps awake grabbing at an unexpected midriff criss-crossed with sutures right beneath his window but when he leans and looks, nothing.

Drench Totems, repulsive sodden effigies slick with wet coral, have erupted helter-skelter from the ruins of buildings, vomiting themselves up through ancient cracks in the pavement surrounded by throngs of paroxysmal hydro-cultists. On the horizon a colossal biomechanical figure half-melted with decay lurches and keens and spews thousands of gallons of black water from its expanse. The tank crew shudder with their bones held close, the driver wiping bloody drool from his mouth with the back of one red hand. In the streets, the alleys, the crack of machine gun fire. In the sky, red lightning.

Ladies and gentlemen, events warrant that MARS associates tune your televisions to no less than sixty-four Central States. If you would kindly prevent at least fifty water sources and Stage Five televisions to your children's mouths, further bulletins will issue your attention. The Metahazard Assault Response Service has issued chronoplastic shutdown. Kindly place all electronics in garbage channel twelve.

In his sockets leaps a wailing whalesong. Sudden sound in his home—he shoots with the tooth of deceased metal. Shaking haze of brackish water screams, "No imprint!" In the night a predator gleaming in his right hand eating with his mouth out his chest.

A woman her shoulder blades strapped to sudden pressure changes. Volkswagen earthquakes, honestly, Springfield the same. Miss Jordan Kent drowned seven squirrels she birthed in the gaps of their skulls black and pitted forward.

The chronoplasmic slug, launched from a Korean smartgun, seeks the shrieking behemoth that lynchpins sea to land and beyond, warping the real into a mouldering stew, the polluted remnants of an ocean's corpse.

The candles in the heads of the Golgotha extinguish in little sprays of black water and Attican rips her hair from her head, beats her breast, screams lamentations to the sky as boiling rain pours down.

Bennett falls backward into the clutching claws of his own ribcage as White Boy straps his gun to his thigh and leaps into a black whirlpool.

The shell strikes the war-titan with a ghastly wrenching sound. The crew clutch their bones close, warding themselves with osteomancies of lost time against a wave of cultists that never comes.

What's the worst that could happen?

ACKNOWLEDGMENTS

This little straight-razor would never have been possible without the attention, efforts, and patience of the inimitable John Skipp, who took a chance on me for which I'm forever grateful. Special notice must be paid to the word "patience", as John stayed with me for four years while I dragged myself through the mud with work in life and in writing—thank you, my brother, for everything from excellent editing and pep talks to solid advice and connecting on common issues. The honor and pleasure are all mine.

Thanks also to Rose O'Keefe, not only for her work giving bizarro a locus, but for her tireless efforts as an independent publisher.

Many thanks to Gabino Iglesias, who took on the unenviable task of translating dialogue into Spanish in Cobra Roja—that story breathes now in a way it couldn't have without you, my dude.

Thanks to Danger Slater, who is always willing to indulge my stress about writing and the ins and outs of an industry I simply do not understand.

Thanks to Anthony, for allowing me use of a computer when I hadn't one of my own—most of these would never have been written without that gracious favor.

My sincerest thanks to Troy, and to Wade, and to Tyler, and to Matt—some of the best friends I'll ever know—who were always excited to hear what I was working on, who fed me new literature and gave me detailed feedback and reassurance and criticism—I wouldn't have built half the universe I have without you.

Thanks of course to The Da, who has been my most consistent and enthusiastic source of encouragement since I was but a lad, who always sends books and voraciously consumes them himself, who gave me my first personal computer and has helped nurture my imagination for decades.

And finally, thank you always to Liz—your determination, intelligence, work ethic, and sense of responsibility urge me every day to strive to be a better person. You give me strength when I have none and always make me laugh. You've abetted my growth as a human being in more ways than I can count and I wouldn't get anything done, never mind a book, without you walking beside me. I love you.

Massachusetts, 2014—North Carolina, 2018

ABOUT THE AUTHOR

S.G. Murphy is a neurotic fiction writer from the eastern continental United States. They once scared themself with a crude ghost costume by cutting holes in a towel and draping it over their head, refusing to look in the mirror.